THE GUNSMITH

451

The Last Way West

THE GUNSMITH

451

The Last Way West

J.R. Roberts

SPEAKING VOLUMES, LLC
NAPLES, FLORIDA
2019

The Last Way West

ISBN 978-1-64540-111-7

Chapter One

INDEPENDENCE, MISSOURI

Wagon trains were extinct.

Well, almost.

The heyday of the trains extended from the 1840s to the 1880s. As the railroads completed their construction, and effectively connected the east to the west, the wagon trains began to die out. It was only certain intrepid souls who still insisted on travelling by wagon train. And those souls needed a Wagonmaster to show them the way.

There weren't many Wagonmasters to be found by the 1880s. The wagon trains that still existed usually elected a Captain, who had very little authority, save for saying when they would stop for the night, and when they would start up again in the morning.

But one Wagonmaster, who seemed to be outlasting all the others was Major Tom Wallace, who happened to have a friend named Clint Adams, also known as The Gunsmith.

***

Arriving just outside of Independence, Mo., Clint Adams was shocked to see a collection of about thirty covered wagons forming a circled camp. Clint knew that wagon trains had long used Independence, Missouri—as well as St. Joseph, Missouri and Council Bluffs, Iowa—as jumping off points from which to head west. But he also knew that the days of wagon trains carrying hundreds of thousands of people across the country were few and far between. Mostly, it was the gold rush in California that drew them. These days, travel by train was cheaper and faster. He knew some people still traveled by wagon train, but it had been quite a while since he had actually seen one.

He was tempted to stop and talk to some of the people, but he had an appointment in Independence that promised to lead to some interesting business, and he didn't want to be late, so he bypassed the train and continued on.

***

Independence had grown since his last visit. He had been to Council Bluffs and St. Joe in recent years, and had seen how those towns had matured, but Independence seemed to have outgrown both of those—at least, to his eye. He certainly had no knowledge of what the active population of any of those towns was.

Clint found a large livery, arranged to board Eclipse, then walked to a nearby hotel and got himself a room. After that, he had a meal in the hotel diningroom, then left the building to find the Golden Gate Saloon, where he was supposed to meet his friend, Bat Masterson.

Masterson had sent a telegram asking Clint to meet him at this location for a "potentially advantageous business deal."

The Golden Gate featured gold batwing doors that led into the large, gold tinged interior. As Clint entered, he wondered if patrons got used to all the gold, or if headaches followed?

He approached the bar, which seemed to be lined with gold leaf. Behind it stood a bartender wearing a white shirt, and a gold vest.

"What can I get ya?" he asked.

"Beer," Clint said, "if it's not gold."

"Nope," the barman said, "same color as always."

He set a beer in front of Clint, and not only was it the usual color, but ice cold.

"Okay?" the bartender asked.

"It's great," Clint said. "Have you seen a dandy in a black suit, a bowler hat, carrying a walking stick?"

"In here?" the bartender said. "Never."

"Okay, thanks."

"For a feller dressed like that, I'd try the Independence Palace."

"A saloon?" Clint asked.

"Saloon, gambling hall, theater and hotel, all in one building," the bartender said. "Takes up a whole entire block."

"Thanks," Clint said, "maybe I'll check that out when I've finished my beer."

"Suit yourself," the bartender said, with a shrug. The man seemed to work in a crouch. Clint had an idea he would be much taller out from behind the bar.

The saloon was doing a brisk business, so the bartender had others to attend to. Clint had some room on either side, but not much. Occasionally, a man on either side would bump him, but so far neither of them had the manors to apologize. They were too busy laughing and drinking with friends. Clint decided to move before somebody got mad.

Maybe Masterson had managed to get to a table without the bartender seeing him. Clint decided to walk around the saloon and take his beer with him.

Chapter Two

The interior seemed as large and spacious as some of the gambling halls Clint had seen in San Francisco. There weren't any house gaming tables, but there were poker games going on. If Masterson was there, he'd be at one of those tables.

Clint walked over, saw five players at each table, but no sign of Bat Masterson. He continued on.

As he walked around, several saloon girls looked him up and down, but only one finally approached him. She was a pretty redhead, tall and lean and freckled. Her green gown made her green eyes stand out.

"You lookin' for a friend, honey?" she asked.

"As a matter of fact, I am," he said.

"Well, I'm pretty friendly," she said.

"I'm sure you are, but I'm looking for a man."

"Oh," she said, obviously disappointed. "You don't appear to be that type."

"I'm not," he assured her. "I'm looking for a friend of mine named Bat Masterson."

Now she looked even more surprised.

"He's a famous man," she said.

"Yes, he is. He probably looks younger than you'd think, well dressed, polite—"

"Polite?" she asked. "We don't see too many of those types in here."

"No, I guess not."

"So, are you a famous man?"

"Some might say that," Clint said, "but I don't want to shout it from the rooftops."

"Well," she said, "if you want me to help you find your friend, I need to know who you are."

He stepped closer to her and lowered his voice.

"My name's Clint Adams."

Her mouth dropped open.

"You're the Gunsmith." She kept her voice as low as his.

"That's right."

"This is so exciting," she said. "The Gunsmith is looking for Bat Masterson."

"Have you seen anybody in here today that might be him?" Clint asked.

"Uh, no," she said. "When were you supposed to meet?"

"Today," Clint said. "But we didn't agree on a time, just a place."

"The Golden Gate?"

"Yes."

"Well . . . I haven't been here all day," she said. "I can ask some of the other girls if they've seen him."

"That'd be good," Clint said. "I can hang around here a bit longer."

"Okay," she said. "Have another beer. Tell Leo, the bartender, that I said it's on the house."

"Really?" Clint asked. "Do you have that authority?"

"I hope so," she said. "My name's Jayne Russell. I own the place."

***

Clint finished his beer while wandering around the room, then worked his way back to the bar and tried out Jayne Russell's name for his free beer.

The bartender set it down in front of him and said, "You met the boss."

"I guess I did."

"She must like you, to buy you a beer," the man said. "She don't give out free drinks."

"Then I'm flattered."

"Here she comes," Leo said. "Be careful."

"Of what?" Clint asked.

"That's all I can say," Leo replied, and moved down the bar.

"Well, I asked the other girls," Jayne Russell said. "Nobody has seen Bat Masterson, or anybody who might look like him."

"Thank you," he said. "And thanks for the free beer. Leo tells me they're rare."

"Oh yeah," she said. "Only famous people drink free here." She leaned on the bar with both elbows. "So what will you do now?"

"I'll go to my hotel," he said. "If Bat couldn't make it, maybe he'll send another telegram."

"Does he know what hotel you'll be in?"

"No," he said, "but if I know Bat, he'll have a copy of the telegram delivered to every hotel."

"Determined man."

"You don't know the half of it."

She stood up straight. She was almost as tall as he was.

"Well, take your time, finish your beer," she said. "Have another, if you like."

"Another free one?"

She laughed.

"Don't push your luck, Mr. Gunsmith."

He laughed and watched as she walked away and blended into the crowd.

Chapter Three

Clint went to his hotel and checked in at the desk to see if he had any messages. The desk clerk looked old enough for this job to have been his life's work.

"Sorry, sir," the clerk said. "I don't have anything."

"Well," Clint said, "if anything does come in, would you bring it right to my room?"

"Of course, sir."

The hotel had rooms available on the ground floor, but Clint had requested one on the second, on the side of the building, where there'd be no access from outside. He didn't need to be worrying about someone coming in his window.

He walked down the hall to room eleven and used his key to enter. Once inside he tossed his hat into a corner, sat on the bed and removed his boots, then hung his gunbelt on the bedpost. That done, he grabbed a wooden chair from the corner and jammed the back of it underneath the doorknob. In effect, the door was now double locked.

Fatigued from his day's ride, he reclined on the bed and stared at the ceiling. He wondered what had kept Bat from meeting him, and hoped his friend was all right.

***

He woke hours later and listened. There was no way hotels could keep their wooden floors from creaking, which was a good thing. To Clint's acute hearing, the sound acted as an alarm to tell him someone was walking in the hall. Very often he'd simply hear someone open the door to their own room and go in. Other times, this didn't happen, so he'd grab his gun from his holster and wait.

This was such a time.

He sat up, swung his feet to the floor, and slid the gun from the holster. Someone was in the hall, and they weren't going to their room.

A knock came.

"Who is it?" he asked.

"The desk clerk, sir," a familiar voice answered. "You requested any message be brought up to you."

Clint opened the door a crack, saw the clerk, and then swung it wide. The clerk took one step back when he saw the gun in Clint's hand.

"Relax," Clint said, "it's just a precaution I take."

"There's a telegram for you, sir," the clerk said, holding it out.

"It came in this late?" Clint asked.

"No, sir, it came this afternoon, but since you weren't a guest yet, it was simply set aside. I found it just a little while ago."

"I see," Clint accepted the telegram. "Thank you."

"Have a good-night, sir."

Clint closed the door, walked to the bed and put the gun back in its holster. Then he sat and rubbed his face vigorously so he'd be awake when he read the message.

As he had suspected and hoped, it was from Bat Masterson. It stated that Bat couldn't be there, he was sorry, something came up, the business matter had somehow faded away, and he hoped to catch up to Clint in the near future. It closed by Bat apologizing again.

Clint refolded the telegram and set it aside.

He knew his friend would not have missed this meeting on a whim. Whatever the "something" was that had come up, had to be important. He would not hold it against Bat, but the fact was he was now in Independence, Mo. for no reason. He could have a good night's sleep, a decent breakfast in the morning, and then saddle up and head west. But just as he had nothing to do in Independence, neither did he have anything to do anywhere else, at the moment. And he hadn't been in this town in some time. He decided to go ahead and have the good night's sleep, and the breakfast, but after that he'd take a look around and spend at least one day there, allowing himself and Eclipse to get some rest.

***

When he woke the next morning, he followed his plan. He had breakfast and took a walk around town, seeing more of the growth in Independence—including a new church, a school, and the new police department.

He recalled seeing all the wagons on the outskirts of town, and assumed that Independence would soon be the jumping off place for at least one more wagon train. He wondered why those people would choose to travel that way when they could have taken a train? Well, to each his own.

When he spotted a buckboard in front of a mercantile and saw how they were loading the back with supplies, he wondered if they were from the wagon train. It was a sure bet that much shopping hadn't been done for a single family.

As he watched, several women came out of the store, followed by a couple of men who were either with them, or simply loading the buckboard for them. The men tossed some sacks onto the back, then waved at the women and walked off. The women went back inside.

Then Clint saw several men who had been watching from across the street leave their vantage point and approach the buckboard.

Chapter Four

As the men began to poke through the supplies in the back of the buckboard, two women came out of the mercantile and stopped short. One of them just stared, but the other one—the younger one—started yelling.

"Hey, what do you think you're doing?"

The four men turned and looked at her, then one smiled as the others went back to looting the wagon.

"We're just pickin' up a few things," he said to her. "You ladies can't really be needin' all this stuff."

"It's not just for us," the woman said. "It's for forty families."

"Forty!" the man said. "Oh, you mean those wagons outside of town?"

"I mean our wagon train," she said.

"Ain't you heard, girlie?" he asked. "Wagon trains are done."

He turned back to the buckboard.

Clint crossed the street as the girl stepped down and tried to stop the men.

"Ellie, don't—" the woman on the boardwalk implored.

The girl didn't listen. She grabbed the arm of the man who had spoken to her and pulled on it.

"Get away from our wagon!"

He turned quickly and backhanded her across the face. She staggered back and fell to the ground.

Clint reached the wagon as the woman looked up from the ground. She saw him, and he realized she was more girl than woman.

"That's enough," he said, grabbing the man's arm.

The man turned his head, saw Clint, sneered and said, "You want some, too?"

He tried to backhand Clint as he had the girl, but Clint ducked and allowed the man to stagger past him. As he did, he planted his foot in the man's ass and shoved. The man ended up sprawled face first in the street.

The other three men stopped what they were doing, stared down at their friend, then looked at Clint.

"You shouldn'ta done that," one of them said.

Clint ignored him, extended his hand down to the girl. She grabbed it and he helped her to her feet. Her clothes were dusty from the street, and she had a bruise forming on her cheekbone, but none of that hid her beauty.

"Thank you," she said. "They were stealing our supplies."

"Yes, thank you so much," the older woman said, stepping into the street and putting an arm around the younger one.

"Are these for the wagon train?" he asked.

"Yes," the younger one said.

"Where are your men?" Clint asked.

"They went to the hardware store," the younger woman answered. "They're going to meet us here."

"If they didn't get lost in a saloon," the older woman growled. She looked to be in her forties, and there was enough alike about the woman to suggest that they were related. They could have been sisters, but Clint thought mother-and-daughter would be more appropriate.

"Look out—" the younger girl started.

"I hear them," Clint assured her.

The man in the street had been helped up by his friends, and then they all turned to face Clint.

Clint turned.

"You made a bad mistake, Mister," said the man whose shirt was dirty from the street.

"Seems to me you're the ones making the mistakes," Clint said. "First trying to steal some supplies, and then knocking this woman down."

"This ain't none of your affair!" the man snapped.

"You made it mine by acting like animals in the street," Clint said.

"Who you callin' animals?" the man demanded.

"Stealing, and attacking a young woman?" Clint said. "That sounds like the actions of animals to me."

"Me, too!" the older woman huffed.

The four men spread out from the buckboard, all with their hands hanging down near their guns.

"Animals don't got no guns," the spokesman of the four said.

"You ladies better go into the store," Clint said.

"You don't have to do this, Mister," the young one said.

"Come on, Ellie," the older woman said. "The man knows what he's doin'."

"But—"

"Come on!"

The older woman literally had to tug the young one off the street and into the store. But their faces soon appeared in one of the windows. Likewise, people on the street had stopped to watch the action.

"What's your name?" Clint asked the spokesman.

"Ben."

"Well Ben, Clint said, "let me teach you animals something."

Chapter Five

"You're gonna teach the four of us somethin'?" Ben asked. "That's a laugh."

"You four fancy yourselves gunmen?" Clint asked. "You can't even keep your guns clean."

"They're clean enough."

"You think so?"

"You're about to find out."

"The supplies in this wagon," Clint asked, "are they enough to die for, Ben? The rest of you?"

"Don't you mean kill for?" Ben said, with a laugh. "Yer so nervous yer usin' the wrong words."

"No," Clint said, "I said 'die' for, and that's what I meant."

The other three men started to look a little unsure, because of Clint's attitude. But Ben was still pretty confident, even after he'd gone sprawling into the dirt.

"Mister," he said, "I think maybe the time for talkin' is over. You either move on or go for that gun."

"Well," Clint said, "I'm not moving, and I'll go for mine when you go for yours, Ben. It's your play."

"Ben—" one of the other men started, but Ben cut him off.

"Shut up!"

A third man said, "They're just supplies, Ben—"

"I said shut up! We're doin' this!"

Clint knew the only way to keep from killing all these men was to either kill one of them quick, or do something that both impressed and frightened them.

So he drew and fired once. Ben's holster flew from his hip, gun and all. He stared down at his hip in shock. There was some residual vibrations there that extended down his leg.

Clint holstered his gun as the mob stared at what he had done.

"Who's next?" he asked.

They all looked at him.

"Or do you want to pick up your gun and try again, Ben?" he asked. "Or borrow a holster from one of your friends?"

Ben looked at Clint, then down at his hip.

"No," he said, then, "forget it. Come on, boys. Let's get a drink."

As the four of them walked away, one asked, "Who is that guy?"

Clint noticed they didn't pick Ben's gun up from the street.

The two women came out of the mercantile, followed by a man wearing a white apron.

"Holy Jesus!" he said. "You're the Gunsmith, ain'tcha?"

"What makes you say that?" Clint asked the man.

"Because I ain't never seen nothin' that fast before," the man said.

"Have you ladies finished with your shopping?" Clint asked. "Or does this man have some more supplies to load into your wagon?"

"No," the older woman said, "we're quite finished, and we have paid the man."

Clint looked at the storekeeper.

"Okay, okay," the storekeeper said, "I'm goin', I'm goin', but . . . sweet Jesus!"

"Are you ladies all right?" he asked.

"We're fine, Mister," the older one said, "thanks to you."

The younger one—who has been called Ellie—looked at Clint with wide, shining eyes and asked. "Are you really the Gunsmith?"

"I'm Clint Adams," he said.

"My God," she said, "we're from back East, and we've heard of you. But I never expected to see—"

"My name is Ada Stevens," the older woman said, "and this is my daughter, Ellie. We thank you kindly for what you've done."

"If you don't mind me asking, what are you ladies doing on a wagon train?" Clint asked. "You could get where you're going by train a lot faster."

"We're following in the steps of those who went before us," Ada Stevens said. "It is our destiny."

Clint had the feeling he was either looking at a couple of Mormon women, or Quakers.

"Are you headed for Utah?" he asked. That would make them Mormons.

"No," Ada said, "we are going to Nevada."

Quakers, then.

And stopping in Nevada would mean they didn't have to brave the treacherous "forty miles of desert," that separated Nevada from California on the California Highway.

"And where are your men?"

"I'm willing to bet they are in a saloon," the older woman said. "Our Wagonmaster's a very bad influence on them."

"You have a Wagonmaster?"

"Indeed," the woman said. "His name is Wallace."

"Major Tom Wallace?" Clint asked, surprised.

"You know him?"

"I do," Clint said. "You've got a good man there. He's been doing this for many years, but I thought he was retired."

"He should retire," Ada said. "Excuse me for saying so, since he is your friend, but I do not think this man should be undertaking such a trek."

"Because of his age?"

"That, and the drinking."

"Drinking?"

"Do you not know that your friend is a drunk?"

"Mother!"

"I know he likes his liquor," Clint said, "but I've never known him to be a drunk—or to be drunk on the job."

"Well, if you go and find him and our men in one of the saloons, I'm sure you'll find him quite drunk, and possibly taking our men right along with him."

"When were you supposed to be leaving?" Clint asked.

"Tomorrow morning," Ada said. "That is why the men sent us here to pick up our supplies."

Clint had never known Tom Wallace to send women to pick up the supplies for one of his trains. He always had men do that kind of work.

He looked around, saw a hotel nearby.

"Ladies," he said, "if you will both go into that hotel and wait in the lobby, I'll see what I can do about finding your men and have them escort you back to the train. And if I don't find them, I'll escort you, myself."

"You're extremely kind, Mr. Adams," Ada said, "extremely kind."

As the ladies went to the hotel, Clint started for one of the saloons, wondering how many it would take before he found the men?

Chapter Six

In the third saloon he tried, he found a group of men standing at the bar, seemingly gathered around one fellow. They were laughing and slapping each other on the back. It was early, and the saloon was not doing a lively business, so the bartender seemed to be paying them special attention.

The saloon was called The Nine of Spades. Clint suspected the card must have had something to do with the ownership of the place. Maybe the owner had won it by filling a straight with that card, or a flush. Saloon names usually had some sort of story behind them.

He moved toward the group, none of whom seemed to be wearing guns. That always screamed Easterner to Clint—either that, or the brand-new trail clothes they seemed to be wearing. Easterners often tried to dress the way they thought "cowboys" would dress.

The man they were gathered around, however, was quite different. His clothes had miles on them, as did his face and the holstered gun on his hip. Major Tom Wallace had started leading wagon trains west in the fifties. He took a break to fight in the Civil War, where he earned the rank of Major. After the war, he went back to being a Wagonmaster.

Clint first met him when he was in his twenties, and actually accompanied him on a couple of treks, acting as a scout. Since then he had only encountered the man a few times, but still considered him a close and longtime friend.

He saw glasses on the bar and in the hands of the men, both beer and whiskey.

The bartender came down to him and asked, "What'll ya have, friend?"

"Beer," Clint said.

The bartender set the cold beer down in front of him.

"You're lucky these jaspers came along when they did, or I might not be open right now."

"I figured," Clint said. "I went to a couple of other saloons, but they were closed."

"They'll all be openin' soon," the bartender assured him. "These ain't the old days, when we could open our doors when we wanted to. Nope, this is a civilized town, now." He said "civilized" like it was a bad word.

"Looks like these fellas are having a high old time," Clint said.

"They're from that wagon train outside of town," the bartender said. "They'll be leaving tomorrow, so they want to get in as much drinkin' as they can today."

"Doesn't sound like a good idea to me," Clint said. "They should be getting their wagons ready."

"Well," the bartender said, "they're here with their Wagonmaster, who looks a little long in the tooth for the job to me. If he don't mind, I guess they don't."

Clint took his beer and moved closer to the group of men. There were four gathered around Tom Wallace.

"Any of you men have wives in town?" Clint called out.

One man turned to face him.

"I do. My wife and my daughter are over at the mercantile. Why, sir?"

"Because I just saved them from four would be gunnies who were trying to steal their supplies."

"Oh Lord," the man said, "Ada will kill me . . ."

"She mentioned something like that," Clint said.

"Hey, fella," Tom Wallace said, turning, "these men are havin' a drink—what the hell. Clint Adams? Is that you?"

"Hello, Major."

"Well, I'll be—" Wallace stumbled back from the bar, pushed away from his group and grabbed Clint in a bear hug.

Always a big, barrel-chested man, Wallace's chest had fallen into his stomach since Clint last saw him. And the man smelled as if he had been drinking for months, not just the morning.

Wallace had him in a tight embrace, and then suddenly the man went limp.

Chapter Seven

"Tom—" Clint said, as the man slumped to the floor.

"What's wrong?" one of the other men asked.

Clint looked at the bartender, the only local man in the saloon, and said, "Get a doctor!"

"Right!"

The bartender ran from the saloon.

"Oh Lord, what can we do?" one of the men asked.

"Help me put him on the bar so the doctor can get to him when he gets here."

All the men helped Clint lift Wallace and lay him on the bar. The man's pallor was gray, and he wasn't looking good.

"Now what?" a man asked.

Clint looked at him.

"Are you Ada's husband?"

"Yes."

"Your wife and daughter are in a hotel lobby across from the mercantile. Go to them. They need you."

"But the Major—"

"There's nothing you can do for the Major, unless you're a doctor," Clint said. "Go!"

As the man started for the door, another man asked, "What can we do?"

"One of you go with him," Clint said, "get the supplies to your wagons."

"Yessir."

A man broke away and followed Ada's husband.

Clint looked at the other two.

"One on either side of him, make sure he doesn't roll off the bar."

"Yessir," they said, and took up the position.

"Does your wagon train have a captain?" Clint asked.

"Yes," one of the men said.

"Is he here?"

"No, he's back at camp."

Good man, Clint thought. Hopefully, Wallace had hired himself a good captain.

Wallace moaned, and the two men grabbed him to keep him from moving.

"What's wrong with him?" one of them asked. "He's not drunk."

"Not drunk?" Clint asked. "He smells pickled."

"To be fair," one of the men said, "he always smells like that."

"Jesus," Clint said.

At that point, the bartender returned with an energetic looking man in his forties, carrying a doctor's bag.

"Move away!" the sawbones said to Clint. "Not you two. Stay there so he doesn't fall."

The doctor looked at Wallace's eyes, took his pulse, opened his shirt.

"What happened here? He smells drunk."

"He just collapsed," Clint said. "One minute he was hugging me tightly, and the next he was limp in my arms."

"Do you know this man?"

"For years," Clint said, "but I haven't seen him in some time."

"And the rest of you?"

"He's our Wagonmaster," one of the men said.

"Drinking heavily?" the doctor asked.

"Yes."

"And at his age—how old is he?" the doctor asked Clint.

"I'm not sure," Clint said. "He could be seventy."

The doctor used his stethoscope, tried what he could, gave Wallace a shot, but in the end, he stepped away, shaking his head.

"This man is dead," he said. "I believe it was a heart attack." He looked at Clint. "I'm sorry for your friend. There was just nothing I could do."

"I understand," Clint said.

"I'm going to need someone to carry him to the undertakers," the doctor said. "I'll lead the way."

"We can do it," the two men from the wagon train said.

One took him under the arms, and the other by the legs, and they carried him out.

Before leaving, the doctor said to Clint, "I think our local law is going to want to talk to you."

"Your sheriff, or new police department?"

The doctor made a face and said, "Police, I'm afraid."

"I'll be around. My name's Clint Adams. Tell them I'll stop in to see them."

"Very well."

When the doctor left the saloon, there was only Clint and the bartender left.

"You didn't have much time with your old friend," the bartender said.

"No, I didn't," Clint said.

"You look like you need a fresh beer."

"And a shot of whiskey," Clint added.

"Comin' up, friend," the barman said.

He set Clint up with the beer and whiskey, then poured a shot for himself.

"Here's to your friend," he said, holding his glass up.

They clinked their glasses and drank.

Chapter Eight

Clint finished his beer and left the saloon as other men started to arrive. The day's clientele was finally putting in their appearance.

Clint went to the undertaker's first, passing the mercantile along the way. The wagon load of supplies was gone, so he assumed Ada's husband had taken it, his wife and his daughter back to their camp.

From there, he went to present himself at the police department. He was interviewed by a lone policeman, who had the doctor's report stating that Wallace had died of a heart attack. Clint told the man what he knew, and that was it. He left and walked back to his hotel, thinking about his friend, Major Tom Wallace. His last wagon train was outside of town. What was going to happen to it? What were all those people going to do?

His hotel had its own saloon attached, so he went to the bar there and had another beer. His stop in Independence was now a complete and utter failure. One friend hadn't arrived when he should've, and another died before they could even reconnect. It was a shame, seeing what Tom Wallace had become, at the end of his life.

With nothing else to accomplish, Clint thought about simply saddling Eclipse and leaving town, but he found it odd to discover that he was hungry. Having Tom Wallace die didn't affect his appetite. What did that say about him as a friend, and as a man?

Possibly just that he was human . . .

***

He was in the middle of his meal when a man entered the restaurant and looked around. Clint had a feeling he knew what—or who—the man was looking for.

Clint had asked the desk clerk in his hotel for a suggestion regarding a restaurant, and the man had sent him there to Hattie's Café. He was assuming the clerk had told this man where to find him.

As the tall, fit looking man approached him, he didn't see a badge on his shirt.

"Mr. Adams?" the man asked.

"That's right."

"I'm sorry to bother you while you're eating," the man said, "but I wanted to catch you before you left town."

"What can I do for you?"

"My name's Lyle Peters," the man said. "I'm the Captain of the wagon train on the outskirts of town. I was working with Major Tom Wallace."

"Ah," Clint said, "I see. Well, have a seat, Mr. Peters, and I'll tell you what I can."

"Actually," Peters said, sitting, "I have all the information I need about what happened to the Major. I talked to the police, and to the doctor."

"Then what more can I do for you?"

"We need a Wagonmaster," Peters said. Clint guessed that the man was only a few years younger than he was.

"But you're the Captain," Clint said. "Can't you take over for the Major?"

"A Captain is not a Wagonmaster," Peters said. "My job is just to make sure everybody's ready to go in the morning, and to get them settled in the evening when we stop. It's the Wagonmaster's job to get us from here to where we're going."

"I spoke to a woman who said you were going to Nevada."

"These people want to go to Reno," Peters said. "And they specifically wanted to go by wagon train. I was hired first, and then I found the Major."

"Tom Wallace should not have been leading any more wagon trains at his age, and in his condition," Clint said.

"I understand that now," Peters said. "As a matter of fact, I suspected it—"

"Suspected?" Clint asked. "You could smell the liquor on him. I don't know how long he'd been drinking like

34

that. He liked his whiskey when I knew him, but this! He wasn't the Tom Wallace I knew."

"Mr. Adams," Peters said, "Tom needed this. He was desperate for it. He said he needed to have one more trip, and this would have been it."

"Then he should've stopped drinking."

"I agree," Peters said, "but he didn't, and he's dead. And all those people are panicking."

"You're going to have to take charge, Peters," Clint said. "Or find yourself another Wagonmaster."

"That's what I'm doing, Mr. Adams," Peters said.

"What? Me?"

"Exactly," Peters said. "Tom Wallace talked about you quite a bit."

"Maybe he did, but he never told you I was Wagon master material."

"He said he knew you as a young man and knew that you'd be able to do anything you wanted in life."

"Mr. Peters," Clint said, "I am definitely not a Wagonmaster."

"I'm really hoping you are, sir."

Chapter Nine

After Clint finished his meal, Lyle Peters said, "Let me buy you a drink and continue to make my case."

"I'll take the drink," Clint said, "but not in the saloon where Tom died."

They walked along for about three blocks before they encountered a small place called Molly's Saloon. Inside they found a woman behind the bar who was built like a mother bear, replete with hairy forearms, but also had a quick smile.

"I'm Molly, boys," she said. "What's your pleasure?"

"Two beers, thank you," Peters said.

"Comin' up!"

As she moved around behind the bar, the peasant blouse she wore gapped and showed breasts like cannon balls bobbing around, threatening to show off her huge nipples. Her age was hard to gauge, but the grey in her hair—both on her head and arms—marked her as at least middle aged.

She set the beers down in front of them and said, smiling, "Put your eyes back in your head, boys. My tits ain't gonna fall out."

"Oh," Peters said, "uh, n, I wasn't—"

"Relax, honey," she said to him. "I'm just funnin' with ya. 'scuse me, I gotta go see to all my other customers."

"All" her other customers was one man at the end of the bar, whose chin was almost inside his beer mug.

"I gotta keep him from drownin'," she laughed, and hurried over to him.

"My God," Peters said, "does she realize how she looks in that outfit?"

"I'm sure she does," Clint said. "The beer's good, though."

"Look, Mr. Adams," Peters said. "I understand you helped Ada Stevens and her daughter, Ellie, this morning."

"That's right, I did."

"Well, you impressed them," he said. "You also impressed her husband and the other men who were in the saloon with the Major. They were all impressed by the way you took charge."

"Doesn't make me a Wagonmaster."

"Mr. Adams, your reputation precedes you. You have been all over this country."

"Still doesn't make me a Wagonmaster."

"Let's make a deal," Peters proposed.

"What kind of deal?"

"Come out to the camp," Peters said. "Talk to the people. Then we'll accept any decision you make."

"I hope you've got one or two other options in mind," Clint said. "Maybe somebody already on the wagon train?"

"Those folks are all Easterners," Peters said. "many of them Quakers."

Ah, he'd been right about that.

"None of them are going to be able to step up and take over," Peters went on.

"They probably expect you to do that," Clint said.

"Then they're gonna be disappointed," Peters said. "I'm a good Captain, but I'd make a terrible Wagonmaster."

"And do you have a scout?"

"We do," Peters said. "A fella named Bob Horton."

"Can't he step up?"

"As you say, he might be an option, but it was agreed that I should approach you, first."

"I don't know . . ."

"We're just asking you to come out, have a look, talk to the people, and then make your final decision."

"You boys ready for another one?" Molly asked.

Clint looked at her with her big smile and hairy arms, then said to Peters, "Sure, let's go."

"Now?" Peters asked.

"Right now!"

***

Out at the camp, Bob Horton was talking to some of the men from the wagon train.

"I know this is gonna come down to a vote of confidence," he told them. "I'm thinkin' I'll be able to count on you gents for your votes."

The half dozen men exchanged glances with each other, and then one said, "Well, sure, Bob, we think you can do the job."

Horton studied the faces of all the men and didn't see the confidence he was hoping for.

"Mr. Cannon," he said to the man who had spoken, "I really appreciate that. I just hope the rest of you feel the same as he does."

Horton was in his thirties, had ridden scout for the army as well as some other wagon trains. He thought this might be his last train, though, and, if he could get the Wagonmaster's pay, it would sure tide him over 'til his next job.

"We'll talk about it, Bob," one of the other men said.

"Sure, Mr. Hope, sure," Horton said. "You all do that. I'll leave you to it."

Horton walked away, wondering who the hell else they might have in mind for the job? He was fairly certain Clint Adams wouldn't take it.

Chapter Ten

Clint saddled Eclipse while Peters waited outside the livery astride his own horse, and then they rode together to the camp.

Nothing had changed since Clint had ridden by on his way to town. The wagons were still circled, and several campfires were burning.

Clint followed Peters into the camp, where they both dismounted. He saw Ada and Ellie Stevens right away, standing in front of their wagon and watching.

"I can have somebody take care of your horse," Peters said.

"He's fine," Clint said. "I don't expect to be here that long."

"That doesn't sound like you're gonna give it much of a chance," Peters said.

"All I meant was, there's no reason to unsaddle my horse," Clint said. "I'll be going back to town."

"Oh, okay."

Peters handed his own reins to another man, who walked the horse away.

"Let's go over to the Major's wagon," Stevens suggested.

"Lead the way."

People watched as they walked through camp, and there was an eerie silence permeating the situation. Of course, they were in mourning for their Wagonmaster, but more than that, were probably wondering if they were ever going to get underway.

They reached a covered Conestoga wagon, where there was a man presiding over a large pot sitting on a fire.

"Mr. Adams, this is Wilkie," Stevens said. "He was the Major's driver and cook."

Wilkie stood, a bandy-legged man who appeared to only be about five-and-a-half feet tall. His face was heavily lined, which effectively hid his age. Could've been forty, or sixty.

"Pleased ta meetcha," the little man said. He stuck his hand out, and when Clint took it, he thought it was the saddest handshake he'd ever had. Wilkie looked like a man about to cry, as he went back to stirring the pot.

"Ah, here comes Bob Horton," Stevens said. "I should warn you, he wants the Wagonmaster job."

"Good," Clint said, "he can have it."

As Horton reached them, Stevens said, "Bob, this is Clint Adams, an old friend of the Major's."

Horton shook Clint's hand and said, "We appreciate what you tried to do for the Major."

"I wish I could've done more."

"So," Horton said, "Lyle says you might be interested in takin' over for Major Wallace."

"He said that, did he?"

"Not true?"

"Lyle is trying to convince me."

"I see. Well, then, I guess I better leave him to it. It was good to meet you. The Major talked about you a lot."

As Horton walked away, Clint had the feeling the man had been too polite.

"Wilkie, give Mr. Adams a cup of coffee," Peters said. To Clint: "I'll collect some of the others."

As the Captain walked away, Wilkie poured Clint a cup of coffee and handed it to him. Clint sipped and nodded approvingly.

"Great trail coffee," he said.

"Thank ya."

Wilkie poured himself a cup, then looked at Clint.

"So you were friends with the Major?" he asked.

"I was. How long were you with him?"

"Over twenty years," Wilkie said. "I think I came in just after you left."

"You've been with him all that time," Clint said. "When did he start drinking so heavily?"

"About ten years ago," Wilkie said. "When he turned sixty, he couldn't handle it. Didn't like gettin' old."

"And when did he get fat?"

"Started at the same time," Wilkie said. "Drinkin' too much and eatin' too much. And he also couldn't handle the wagon trains becoming unnecessary."

"I always knew Major Tom Wallace to be a strong, smart leader," Clint said.

"The strength went away with age," Wilkie said. "The smarts with the drinkin'."

"Why did you stay with him?"

"He wouldn't have been able to get through a day without me," Wilkie said.

"If that's true," Clint said, "why don't you take over as Wagonmaster and lead these people where they want to go?"

"They wouldn't follow me," he said. "To them I'm just a cook."

"What about Horton?"

"He wants to lead, but he doesn't have what it takes."

"And Lyle?"

"He might be able to do it if he believed it," Wilkie said. "No, I think the one to lead these people is you, Mr. Adams. You knew the Major, you knew his ways."

"I knew his ways thirty years ago," Clint said.

"Well," Wilkie said, "those are the ways that are gonna get these people to Reno."

Chapter Eleven

"This is not gonna be a hard journey," Wilkie said. "They don't wanna go all the way to California. So no forty miles of desert, and no treacherous mountain passes."

"All the more reason you should do it," Clint said.

"Not a chance," Wilkie said. "Besides, if I become Wagonmaster, who's gonna cook? Look, the Major really wanted this. He wanted to take these people to Reno, and then he was gonna retire."

"To do what?"

"He said he was gonna lose weight, stop drinkin', and buy a ranch."

"Not a chance," Clint said. "Tom Wallace was not a rancher."

"I know that," Wilkie said. "I think he was gonna guide this wagon train, and then just die."

"Suicide?" Clint asked.

"One way or another," Wilkie said. "Drink himself to death, or put a bullet in his brain."

Clint was considering what Wilkie said when Lyle Peters returned, leading a line of men. As they approached, Clint counted twelve.

"Gents, this is Clint Adams."

Clint recognized the four men who had been in the saloon with Wallace, including Ada Stevens' husband. He was a tall, bearded man with a mostly baldpate.

"Mr. Adams," he said, extending his hand, "I'm Abraham Stevens. I'd like to formally thank you for what you did for my wife and daughter."

"I was happy to help," Clint said. "I hope all the supplies got to camp intact."

"They did," Stevens said. "My wife and daughter would like you to stop by our wagon before you leave, no matter what you decide."

"I'll do that, Mr. Stevens."

"The rest of these gents have all decided they want to offer you the position of Wagonmaster."

"Do you all represent everyone on the train?"

"Most of them," Peters said. "Some of them have decided to leave the train, some of them want to give the job to Horton."

"We represent the majority, Mr. Adams," Abraham Stevens said. "You knew the Major, and we want you."

"What you folks have to understand," Clint said, "is that this is not what I do."

"We do understand," Stevens said. "We just ask that you walk the train, talk to the people, and then decide."

The men behind him all nodded their heads, and a couple of them said, "Please."

"All right," Clint said, "let's take a walk."

***

Clint walked the train with Lyle Peters and Abraham Stevens. The other men went to their own wagons to wait for him.

As he passed each wagon, the people either spoke to him, reached out to him or—in rare cases—ignored him. A few of the people were obviously packing to leave the train.

"Where are they going?" Clint asked Peters and Stevens. "Back where they came from, or on to Reno on their own?"

"That'll be up to each of them individually," Peters said. "So far they haven't told us."

"How many wagons do you have? And how many are pulling up stakes?"

"We had forty," Stevens said. "So far five are pulling out. Ah, and here's mine."

Like most of the wagons, it was a covered Conestoga with a fire going alongside it. Ada and Ellie smiled as he approached.

"Mr. Adams," Ada greeted.

"Hi," Ellie said, her eyes shining brightly.

"Hello, ladies," Clint said. "I think after all we've been through, you better call me Clint."

"Would you like coffee, Clint?" Ellie asked.

"I had some of Wilkie's coffee," he said.

"Oh," she said, "ours isn't as strong."

"That's okay," Clint said. "I've got other wagons to see."

"Are you going to help us, then?" Ellie asked.

"That's still to be determined, Ellie," Lyle Peters said.

"Well, I hope you will," Ada said. "We would happily put ourselves into your hands."

Ada looked different somehow, younger on this night, and prettier, with her hair done less severely. She was wearing a simple dress that hugged her womanly figure. Ellie had a similar dress on and, in her twenties, was much more slender than her mother, who was at least twenty years older than she was.

"Why don't we move on?" Peters suggested.

"I'll stay here with my wife and daughter," Abraham Stevens said.

"Fine," Peters said, and he and Clint moved on.

***

"Did you both have to wear those dresses?" Abraham demanded when the two men were out of earshot.

"We were just trying to look nice, Abraham," Ada Stevens said.

"Yes, for him?" Abraham demanded, pointing at the Gunsmith's retreating back.

"We need him," Ada said.

"Yes," Abraham said, "*we* need him. All of us! Not just you."

"Don't be crude," Ada said, and stalked away from her husband.

Ellie sniffed and followed her mother.

Chapter Twelve

When Clint and Lyle Peters got to the last wagon, Clint was surprised to see that there was only one woman there.

"Miss Rogers? This is Clint Adams. Clint, this is Delilah Rogers."

The woman was auburn-haired, tall and bosomy, which the man's clothing she was wearing couldn't hide. Her hair tumbled down over her shoulders in waves.

"Ah," she said, putting her hands on her hips, "the man who's going to get us to Reno?"

She breathed deeply, swelling her breasts, and stared at him boldly. The woman was definitely not a Quaker. What was she doing on this wagon train? And alone?

"That hasn't been decided, yet," Clint said. "If you don't mind me saying so, Ma'am, you don't seem to fit here with all these other folks."

"That's because they're all nice, God-fearing people," she said. "I'm not. I'm going to Reno to open a saloon."

"Traveling alone? The last wagon?"

"I'm the last wagon because none of these other nice people want to be near me," she said. "Especially the women. They're all hoping I'll fall behind and get lost, at some point."

"Doesn't make them sound as nice as you said," he commented.

"Well," she said, "if you take over this wagon train, you'll find out who's nice and who's not."

Clint looked at Peters.

"The Major was going to let a woman travel alone?"

"But I'm not alone," Delilah Rogers said. "I have all these people with me—even if they won't look at me."

"And you're still going?" Clint asked. "Even without the Major?"

"I don't have much choice," she said. "I have nowhere else to go."

"You can't go back?"

"I'm not gonna tell you where I came from, but no, I can't go back," she said. "They would've driven me out on a rail if I had the money for a train ticket."

"So you're on a wagon train."

"That's about the size of it."

"Well . . . I wish you luck," Clint said.

"If we don't have you to replace the Major," she said, "we're gonna need it!"

"I'll let you know what he decides," Peters said. "Why don't we go back to the Major's wagon?"

Clint looked at Delilah Rogers, touched the brim of his hat, and followed Lyle Peters away.

***

When they reached the head wagon, Clint asked, "So whose wagon will this be, now?"

"Yours. If you take the job," Peters said.

Wilkie greeted each man with a cup of trail coffee.

"Thanks," Peters said. He turned to Clint. "So, what do you think?"

"I think I want to see the inside of this wagon," Clint said.

"All the Major's stuff is in there," Wilkie said. "I can clean it out, if you decide to join us."

"We'll see," Clint said.

He went to the wagon, still carrying his coffee cup, and climbed into it.

It certainly was Major Wallace's wagon. His Civil War cutlass was hanging on the side, along with his old hat, and his service revolver. There was a large chest, and when Clint opened it, found it held many more mementoes.

He closed the trunk and sat on it. This was Major Tom Wallace's last wagon train. Usually, when a train was leaving Independence for California, you could figure on it taking months. Some of that time would be cut off since they were only going as far as Reno. But it would still take up a lot of Clint's time, and did he want to devote that much of his life to this one undertaking?

Tom Wallace was going to be buried in Independence, where he had spent much of his life preparing to travel west. Allowing this wagon train to fall apart was no kind of remembrance to the man. He didn't want people's last thought of Wallace to be a drunken old man who left them with their butts hanging in the wind.

And he had to admit, the presence of Delilah Rogers on the train made the undertaking a little more attractive. But it would take more than a sexy woman to get him to commit that much of his time to any kind of endeavor.

Tom Wallace's belongings began to close in on him, and he felt himself in need of some space. As he stepped out of the wagon, both Lyle Peters and Wilkie looked over at him.

"Well?" Peters asked. "Have you decided?"

"God help me," Clint said, "but for the benefit of Major Tom Wallace's memory, I'll do it."

"Yes!" Peters said, punching the air.

"But it has to be done my way," Clint said.

"Of course," Peters said. "What's first?"

"Wilkie," Clint said, "I'm going to take you up on your offer to clean out that wagon, but just see how much of what's hanging on the side you can fit into that trunk."

"I'll get it all in," Wilkie said, "you can count on that."

Chapter Thirteen

Clint had to go back to town to arrange for Tom Wallace's burial, to collect whatever supplies he deemed necessary for the trip, and to take care of his hotel room and livery stable costs.

He decided to spend one more night in the hotel and ride out to the wagon train in the morning. Then he would take the entire day to make sure everyone was ready for the trip, and they'd leave the morning after.

If he was going to ride from Independence to Reno, he knew how he would go. But taking thirty-five or forty wagons on that trek was quite different. In the old days of wagon trains, a lot of the trip would be made over previously untraveled ground. But now, at least some of the trip would actually be made on established roads. Or he could even follow the permanent ruts in the ground that had been left behind by years of wagon wheels.

When he got back, he still had time to go to the undertaker's and pay the man to bury Tom Wallace.

"Will you be attending the burial?" the man asked.

"I doubt it," Clint said. "I hate watching my friends being planted in the ground."

"Well," the undertaker said, "if you change your mind, I'll be doing it tomorrow morning."

"I'll keep that in mind," Clint told him.

"Would you like to see your friend one last time?" the undertaker asked. "He's in the back."

"No, thank you," Clint said. "I'd prefer to remember him the way I knew him years ago, not the way he looks now."

"Understood, sir. I'll take good care of him."

"I know you will," Clint said, "because I'll be checking. Understand?"

"Yessir!"

Clint left the undertaker's as dusk began to fall. He found himself hungry, went back to the last café he had eaten in to have supper. Breakfast the next morning would be his first meal as a Wagonmaster.

***

Clint managed to get to the mercantile just in time to load his saddlebags with the things he wanted for the trip. Anything else would have to come from the wagon train's supply wagon, but he needed his own ammunition, his own beef jerky, some extra underwear and a few other items.

He managed to get his saddlebags packed and cinched when there was a knock on his door. He tossed the saddlebags into a corner, walked to the door, still wearing his gunbelt.

"Who is it?" he asked through the door.

"Delilah Rogers," a woman's voice said. "We met this afternoon."

He opened the door a crack, saw that she was alone, and then swung it wide.

"Miss Rogers."

"Please," she said, "call me Delilah." She was dressed as she had been when he saw her earlier, but her hair looked and smelled cleaner. "May I come in?"

"If you're not worried—"

"—about my reputation?" she finished. "Please, I stopped worrying about that a long time ago."

"Then by all means, come in."

He stepped back and allowed her to enter.

"You probably know why I'm here," she said.

"They sent you to talk me into taking the Wagonmaster job," Clint said.

"Is that what you think?"

"And I don't blame them," Clint went on. "After all, you're the most interesting person on that wagon train."

"Do you really think so?"

"I know so," Clint said. "Remember, I walked that whole train and met all the people."

She smiled.

"I understand your thinking," she said. "Most of them are Quakers."

"And it doesn't seem as if everyone on the train is of one mind," he went on. "Some want me, some want Horton. The question is, does Horton want the job?"

"Oh, he wants it," Delilah said. "He wants it very much. In fact, he wants quite a few things he can't have."

"Like what?"

"Like me, for instance," she said.

"Well," Clint said, "I can understand that."

"That's what I came here to talk to you about," she said.

"Has he been bothering you?" Clint asked. "Do you want me to—"

"No, no, no, it's nothing like that," Delilah insisted. "I came here to talk about us."

"Us?"

"Come on," she said, "you know you took one look at me, and I took one look at you, and if we were alone, we would've torn each other's clothes off."

"Delilah—"

"Well," she said, unbuttoning her shirt, "we're alone now."

Chapter Fourteen

"Wait," Clint said.

She stopped after only two buttons.

"What's wrong?"

"You said something about taking each other's clothes off," he reminded her. "In fact, I think you said . . . tearing."

She stepped closer to him and started to unbutton his shirt.

"I don't know about you," she said, "but I don't have so much in the way of clothes that I can afford for you to literally tear them off. But this . . ." She slid her hands inside his shirt, ". . . can be just as effective."

As she slid his shirt off, he removed his gunbelt and hung it on the bedpost. Then he turned his attention to her, unbuttoning her shirt the rest of the way, then sliding it off. He tossed it aside and stepped back. They were now both naked to the waist.

As he expected, her breasts were full, with heavy undersides, and nipples the color of rust.

"Can I help you with your boots?" he asked.

"Please."

Once they had her boots off, they worked on his. After that came their trousers, and then they were naked.

"Now this is what I had in mind," she said, stepping closer to him. "The men on that wagon train are a bore. Other than that, their wives wouldn't let them come near me, anyway."

"I don't blame them," Clint said. "The wives, I mean. If those men saw what I'm seeing now, they'd never let you alone."

"I'm flattered," she said. "If the women saw what I'm seeing . . ." She reached out and stroked his penis, which began to thicken.

He reached out and cupped her breasts, then ran his hands down her body, enjoying the smooth and hot feel of her skin on his palms. Slowly he slid one hand between her legs, probed with his fingers and found her wet. Her body jerked when he first touched her, but then she sighed and closed her eyes as he stroked her. At the same time, she closed her hand on his cock and pulled on it. They continued to stand close together, rubbing and touching each other until she shuddered and made a sound deep in her throat.

"Omigod," she said. "My legs . . ." She closed her eyes.

"Let's go to bed," he suggested.

She opened her eyes and said, "Oh, yes."

Still holding each other they gravitated to the bed and then slid onto it . . .

***

Wilkie handed Lyle Peters a plate of beef stew he'd made in a huge pot, and a cup of coffee. He then did the same for Bob Horton, and himself. They sat around the fire and ate.

"So whataya think?" Wilkie asked.

"About what?" Peters asked.

"About having the Gunsmith as our Wagonmaster. Do you think he can do the job?"

"No," Horton said.

"Yes," Peters said. "I think he can do it. Major Wallace talked about him a lot."

"Yeah," Wilkie said, "when he was a young man, and a scout. Now he's older, and you want him to suddenly be a Wagonmaster."

"What about you, Horton?" Peters asked. "You suddenly want us to believe you can be a Wagonmaster? After all, you've been a scout for years."

"Look," Horton said, "when the Major died, I was willing to step up and fill the void."

"And if something happens to Adams," Peters said, "before or after we leave, we may ask you to do the same thing."

"And I'll be ready," Horton said.

"Excuse me?"

All of the men looked up at the woman who had just entered their camp. Her name was Elizabeth Landers, and she was perhaps the only friend Delilah Rogers had on the wagon train.

"Miss Landers," Peters said, standing. The other two men followed. "Can we do something for you?"

"Mr. Peters, I can't find Delilah."

"Miss Rogers?" Horton said. "Is she missing?"

"I wouldn't say she's missing," Liz Landers said. "Her horse is gone, too. I believe she rode off."

"She left the train?" Wilkie asked.

"No," Liz said, "I don't think she'd leave her entire wagon behind. I think she rode into town, and I'm worried."

"Into town?" Peters asked.

"Yes," she said, "to see Clint Adams. He's a dangerous man, isn't he?"

"Yes," Horton said.

"No," Peters said, "he's a man who's going to help us."

"Well, Delilah said she thought she could convince him to agree to take the job."

"But," Peters said, "he's already agreed."

"He has?" Liz asked. "Then why would she go to town to see him?"

"I guess," Peters said, "we'll have to ask her when she comes back."

"If she comes back," Wilkie said.

"I'll ride in and find her," Horton said.

"No," Peters said, "I want everybody to stay in camp tonight."

Horton had started to walk away, and now he turned to face Lyle Peters.

"Who left you in charge?"

Peters turned and faced him.

"Until we have a new Wagonmaster," he said, "I'm the Captain, and I *am* in charge. Nobody leaves camp."

"But Delilah did leave," Horton said.

"And she'll be back," Peters said, "probably in the morning with Clint Adams. Now, why don't you walk Miss Landers back to her wagon?"

"Yeah, sure."

"And don't leave camp, Horton!" Peters yelled to the man's retreating back.

Horton waved without looking back.

"Where do you think the woman went?" Wilkie asked.

"I saw something pass between her and Adams this afternoon," Peters said.

"So you think she went to town to . . . spend the night with him?"

"That's what I think."

Wilkie grinned and said, "Lucky damn Gunsmith."

Chapter Fifteen

The bed creaked beneath their combined weight as Clint and Delilah rolled around on it together. Clint found her to be one of the more solid women he had ever been with. Her skin was smooth, with absolutely no mushy, soft areas. Even her belly—where some women first began to show their age—was flat and taut. And yet she was at least in her mid-thirties, which probably put her squarely in-between Ada Stevens and her daughter, Ellie.

Clint had some questions for her, but that would come later. At the moment, he was enjoying every inch of her, front to back, top to bottom, rolling her over so he could explore all of her with his mouth and hands.

When he finally settled in with his face between her legs, he worked her with his tongue until she screamed . . . and then she took her turn . . .

***

Wilkie handed Lyle Peters another cup of coffee, sat back down with one of his own.

"How do you see this playin' out?" he asked.

"I think Adams will get us where we're going," Peters said.

"How do you think everyone will react?" Wilkie asked. "So many of these people signed up *because* the Wagonmaster was Major Tom Wallace. Right now we've got five or six pullin' out, and they're gonna want some money back. If more decide to go their own way—"

"They won't," Peters said. "I've talked to almost everybody on the train. I might have even convinced one or two not to leave."

"By tellin' them the Gunsmith will take us safely to Reno?" Wilkie asked.

"Wilkie," Peters said, "we both know that the only reason the Major agreed to make this trip was because you and me were going to be holding him up. Now with Adams, we don't have that responsibility."

"Yeah," Wilkie said, "but will he know what he's doin'?"

"Maybe not every step of the way," Peters said, "but that's where you and me, we'll still come in."

"And what about Horton?"

"What about him?" Peters asked. "He'll do his job."

"You don't think he's gonna have it out with Adams sooner or later?"

"He's a scout, not a gunman," Peters said. "He may have wanted to step up and be Wagonmaster, but he's not going to be willing to fight the Gunsmith for the spot."

"And what about Delilah Rogers?" Wilkie said "We both knew she was gonna be our other problem. The men on this train are tripping over their tongues, and the women probably want her dead or gone."

"If she did leave town to go visit Adams in his room," Peters said, "then she's taken care of. She's got no interest in the men on this train, least of all the Quakers."

"And Horton?"

"He's interested in her," Peters said, "not the other way around. And even if she would've ended up sleeping with him on the trip, that's not going to happen anymore."

"And you don't think Adams will be a problem for us?" Wilkie asked.

"He might even be less of a problem than the Major would've been," Peters said. "After all, he's going to be real busy."

"I hope you're right," Wilkie said. "The last thing I want is to have the Gunsmith figure out what we're hauling across the country."

"Don't you worry," Peters said. "Everything is going to work out for us. You'll see,"

"I hope you're right," the cook said.

Chapter Sixteen

Delilah got Clint settled on his back, and then just roamed his body with her lips and tongue. When she reached his penis, it was tree-trunk hard, and yet she still teased it with her fingertips and the tip of her tongue before taking it completely into her mouth. Clint had to gasp as she started bobbing her head, sliding her lips up and down, and moaning while she sucked him.

The suction of her mouth was incredible, one moment her lips were just gliding over him, and the next she was tugging on him. When he finally couldn't hold it in anymore, he exploded and she moaned and took it all . . .

***

"This trip is going to be a lot more interesting than I thought," she said later, as they lay side-by-side in bed. He was running the fingers of his left hand through her pubic patch, while she was stroking his semi-hard cock with her right.

"It would have been an interesting trip no matter what," Clint said.

"Oh, I told you about those men," she said. "And their women. Now, at least, with you along I'll have somebody to . . . talk to."

"Are you telling me you don't have one friend on that wagon train?"

"Well," she said, "maybe one. Her name's Liz Landers. She's also traveling alone, so we sort of . . . bonded."

"Well, that was good."

"So now I'll have two friends." She tightened her hand on him. "But only one really close friend."

She was wet. He slid a finger into her, making her even wetter. She moaned and rolled over on top of him, maintaining her hold on his cock, which was now fully hard. She straddled him, pressed the head of his penis to her wet vagina lips, and then shimmied down on him, taking him into her steamy depths.

And then she started to ride . . .

***

Abraham Stevens met Bob Horton behind his wagon. His wife and daughter were inside, so they had to keep their voices down.

"You weren't very helpful," Horton said. "You said you'd back me."

"What could I do alone?" Stevens asked. "The others have seemed to change their minds, now that Clint Adams is in the picture."

"So he's a legend," Horton said. "So what? Does that mean he can be a Wagonmaster?"

"Some of the others think he's at least as qualified as you are," Stevens said.

"Well, they're gonna find out they're wrong," Horton said. "And when he falters and falls, I'll be there." Horton poked Stevens in the chest. "And you better be there, too."

"Are you threatening me?" Stevens asked.

"I'm just telling you," Horton said, "that you better keep your part of the bargain."

With that, Horton turned and walked away.

***

Inside the wagon Ada and Ellie Stevens exchanged a look. Although the men were keeping their voices down, the women had heard every word.

"What bargain are they talking about, Ma?" Ellie asked.

"I don't know, dear," she said, "but I don't like the sound of it. Now that we have Mr. Adams, I truly feel we're going to get to Reno. Unless your father and Mr. Horton do something foolish."

"Should we warn Mr. Adams?" Ellie asked.

"We would be going against your father," Ada said, "but I think we might have to."

***

Later Clint asked, "Will you be going back to camp tonight?"

"In the dark? I think my horse is liable to break his leg. No, I was hoping you wouldn't put me out after you were done with me."

Clint rolled onto his side and put his hand on her stomach, rubbing it gently.

"What makes you think I'm done with you?"

She rolled into him and said, "That's what I was hoping you'd say."

Chapter Seventeen

Clint and Delilah rode to the wagon train camp together the next morning. Before they reached it, though, Clint stopped their progress and said to Delilah, "Why don't you just go ahead and ride up to your wagon. Then I'll ride in."

"Don't want to rub our love into anybody's face, huh?" she asked, laughing so he would know she was kidding. "Okay, Clint. I'll see you later. When do you think we'll be pulling out?"

"Not 'til tomorrow morning," Clint said. "I have a lot of work I need to get done.

"Like what?"

"I want to check everyone's wagon and horses," Clint said. "I don't want any breakdowns right at the beginning of our trip."

"I get it," she said. "So I'll see you when you come to check my wagon."

Clint nodded, and Delilah rode ahead of him. He gave her a good head start, and when he felt she was in place, rode into camp, himself.

"'mornin'," Wilkie greeted him. The man was standing over the fire.

"Good-morning," Clint said, dismounting. "Who takes care of the horses?"

"We got a fella named Mike Rowland does that."

"Get him for me, will you?"

"Sure thing. That's quite a horse you got there."

"Let's see if Rowland can handle him."

"He should be able to," Wilkie said. "The Major picked him out, himself."

"Then this'll be interesting," Clint said.

Wilkie went to get Mike Rowland, while Lyle Peters came from the other direction.

"'mornin', Clint," he said. "Wanting to get an early start?"

"I don't see us leaving until tomorrow morning, Lyle," Clint said.

"So, what do you want to do today?" Peters asked.

"I'd like to look over everyone's wagon and team," Clint said.

"The Major did that already," Peters said.

"The Major wasn't himself," Clint said. "I'd like to take a look myself."

"Well," Peters said, "I can tell you learned from the Major. Sure, we can do that. Want to start now?"

"As soon as I see if this Mike Rowland can handle my horse."

"Mine's good with horses," Peters said, "but that animal of yours is special."

Wilkie returned at that moment, leading a man in his forties who was bow-legged, and missing a couple of fingers. Clint immediately felt that the man was a competent horseman. Who else would keep working with horses after having fingers bitten off.

"Wow," Rowland said, looking at Eclipse. "Hey, big boy, how are you?"

Rowland stood in front of the big Darley and the animal nodded his head at him and allowed him to take up his reins.

"You're Mr. Adams?" Rowland asked.

"I am."

"Well," Rowland said, "I'm gonna take good care of this fella."

"I know you will," Clint said. "So now I can concentrate on other things."

Rowland walked the big Darley away.

Clint turned to Peters and said, "Okay, let's get on with this."

They started walking from wagon to wagon, with Clint examining the Conestogas and teams that would be pulling them.

Clint found most of the wagons to be in perfect order. Two or three looked to need some work on their axles, but that could be taken care of during the course of the day. There were also a couple that needed to have wheels replaced, which could also be done that day. It didn't look like there was anything that would keep them from leaving the next morning.

When he got to the Stevens wagon, he had Abraham, Ada and Ellie step down so he could inspect it.

"We're so happy that you decided to lead us," Ellie told him.

Clint noticed Abraham giving his wife and daughter dark looks while he was there. He examined their wagon inside and out, and then the two horses that would be pulling it.

"The mares have to be at least eight years old," Clint observed.

"This is Trixie," Ada said, stroking the neck of one, "and she's eight, but Dixie is nine."

"Trixie and Dixie?"

"I named them," Ellie said, "when I was thirteen."

"Do you have a problem with these horses?" Peters asked.

Clint ran his hands along the flanks, and up and down the legs of the horses.

"I thought I might, but they seem very fit."

"I take good care of these animals," Abraham said.

"Yes, you do," Clint said, "and I commend you for it."

Abraham seemed mollified by that, and his look seemed to brighten a bit.

"Thank you," he said.

"Do we have your approval?" Ada asked, staring at him so intently that he thought she might be trying to send him a message of sorts.

"You do," Clint said.

"Oh, thank you," Ellie said, clapping her hands.

"We have a few more," Peters said. "And then maybe you'd like to eat with us?"

"Is Wilkie's food as good as his coffee?" Clint asked.

"It's better."

"All right, then," Clint said, "let's get those last few done."

The next wagon was fine, and then they got to the next to last one, before Delilah's, which belonged to her friend, Elizabeth Landers.

"So you're Clint Adams," the woman said.

"That's me," Clint said. "And you're Liz."

Liz had an earthy appeal that, at thirty or forty, worked for her. She was wearing a dress that appeared to be shapeless, yet there was a hint beneath it that she wasn't. She had a ready smile, and bright eyes in a face that looked as though she had lived a hard life.

"I am," she said, "and I'm happy that you agreed to help us after the poor Major's passing, Mr. Adams."

And I understand you're Delilah's only friend on this train," Clint commented.

"I think that's because I'm the only person—man or woman—who doesn't feel threatened by her. But," she went on, "from what she told me today, I guess I'm not her only friend, any longer."

"No, you're not."

"So, I think that makes us friends, too?"

"It does," Clint said, "and that means you have to call me Clint."

"And you call me Liz," she said. "You want to take a look at my wagon?"

"That's what I'm here for."

"Be my guest, then."

He examined the outside of her wagon, then ran his eyes and hands over her team. They were a couple of five-year-old geldings, probably two of the best horses he'd seen.

"And would you like to come inside?" she asked.

The look on her face told him that if he went inside her wagon, he might not come out for a while.

"I don't think I need to do that, Liz," he said. "Your rig is in perfect condition."

"Yes, it is, honey," she said.

Peters had been standing off to one side, and now he came forward and said, "One last wagon, Clint."

"See you later, Liz," Clint said.

"See you later, scaredy-cat."

Chapter Eighteen

Delilah was waiting when they reached her wagon.

"You survived Liz," she said to Clint.

"I did," he said. "She tried to get me to come inside her wagon, but I resisted."

"Hello, Miss Rogers."

"Mr. Peters," Delilah said, "thank you for coming by."

"We're just here so Clint can check your rig," Peters said.

"I understand."

Clint walked around her wagon, took a look inside, then examined her team.

"It all looks good," Clint said.

"Thank you," she said.

"We'll be leaving in the morning, Miss Rogers," Peters said. "Please be ready."

"Oh, I will be," she said. "I'm always ready."

Clint and Peters headed back to the lead wagon.

"Just get those axles and wheels fixed and we'll be ready to go," Clint said.

"I'll have our men work with each individual wagon, so we'll be ready."

When they reached the front wagon, Wilkie started to fill plates for them.

Clint and Peters accepted their food and settled down around the fire to eat.

"This is really good," Clint said. "What is it?"

"It's rabbit, but I prepared it in a way only I know," Wilkie said.

"I guess you did," Clint said, "because I wouldn't have picked this out as rabbit."

"And it's only lunch," Wilkie said. "There'll be something a bit more for supper."

"Then I better work up an appetite," Clint said. He looked at Peters. "I want to work on those axles with your men and the individual wagon owners. It'll give me a chance to get to know everyone."

"That sounds like a good idea," Peters said. "The Major made sure we had a couple of men on the train who could do most types of repairs, if necessary."

"He always was a smart man."

"He still was," Peters said. "He lost some of what he had, but he still had that."

They washed down their lunch with some of Wilkie's good trail coffee. When they were done, they both stood up.

"Time to get to those repairs," Clint said.

"We'll meet the men at the first wagon," Peters said.

Chapter Nineteen

Clint worked with two men named Dave and Chuck, fastening wheels and tightening axles until all the wagons were ready for the trip.

The work was done just in time for Clint to clean up and then join Lyle Peters, Bob Horton and Wilkie at the campfire for supper.

While they ate—a loaded beef stew, which seemed to be Wilkie's specialty—Peters said, "Well, so far our people are saying good things about you. I don't think they expected the Wagonmaster to be working on their wagons."

"These people are going to have to know that they can depend on me, no matter what."

Horton remained silent, listening while he ate. He didn't look like a happy man.

"Well, so far that's the case," Peters said.

They washed down their meal with coffee, and then Wilkie gave them each a final cup while he cleaned up. He had obviously spiked the coffee, this time, with a touch of whiskey, but neither man complained.

"Do you have any family?" Clint asked Peters. "A wife? Kids?"

"No," Peters said, "that's why I took a job like this, traveling west. I'm not leaving anybody behind."

"How about you, Horton?" Clint asked. "Any family?"

"Nobody." He didn't offer more than that.

"And you?" Peters asked. "No family anywhere?"

"No," Clint said. "I've never settled into one spot long enough for that."

"I guess we have that in common, then," Peters said. He looked over at Horton. "The three of us."

"And what about Wilkie?" Clint asked.

Peters looked over at the small man who was cleaning out his pots and plates.

"Wilkie's got a wife, somewhere," Peters said. "But I think he takes jobs like this to get away from her for a while."

"Maybe that's how he stays married," Clint said, "taking a break every once in a while."

"Everybody's got their own ways," Peters said. "Me, I don't think I could live with someone else—least of all a woman."

"Why's that?"

"I don't understand women," Peters said. "They confound me."

"Well," Clint said, "I can't argue with you, there. They pretty much confound me, too."

"Not according to your reputation."

"Reputations are so exaggerated, Lyle," Clint said.

I hope not," Peters said.

"Why's that?"

"I'm counting on your reputation to get us from here to Reno safely."

"You'd be better off counting on me, and not on my reputation for that," Clint said. "By the way, I just came up with a question."

"What's that?"

"I haven't seen any children on this train."

"There are none," Peters said. "Some of these folks are too old to have kids, others are waiting to get to their new homes to start a family."

"Well, I can't say I'm disappointed," Clint said. "It'll be a lot easier trip without kids."

"I think that's what the Major was figuring," Peters said. "He turned away some families with kids. He suggested that they take the train."

"I'm still puzzled as to why all these people would travel this way," Clint said. "I know Ada Stevens said something about following in the steps of those who went before, but—"

"She and many of the others feel that way," Peters said. "I know they don't mean ancestors. Nobody's going back that far. But there were other family members who made the trip. I think they hope to find them when we get there."

"What about letters?" Clint asked. "Haven't they exchanged mail?"

"No."

"So they're travelling there on faith?"

"I guess you could say that."

"Geez," Clint said. "I wish I had that much faith in . . . well, anything."

"More coffee?" Wilkie asked, walking over with the pot.

"Oh, yes," Clint said.

"With a sweetener?" the man asked, taking a bottle of whiskey from his pocket.

"Definitely," Peters said, holding out his cup.

***

Delilah Rogers and Liz Landers sat around a fire next to Delilah's wagon. They had just finished their supper and were also drinking coffee—without whiskey.

"He's handsome," Liz said.

"Yes, he is," Delilah said.

"Was he good?"

Delilah smiled and said, "Very."

Liz smiled back.

"Are you gonna share?"

"Oh, yes!"

Chapter Twenty

"As far as sleeping," Wilkie said, "the wagon's yours."

"That's okay," Clint said. "I'll bunk under the wagon. If you want, you can sleep inside."

"I think we both have the same problem with that," the cook said.

"The Major," Clint said.

Wilkie nodded.

"I'll sleep over there." The cook pointed.

"And Peters?"

"He's got a bedroll near here," Wilkie said.

"So I guess we better get some rest," Clint said. "We'll want to get an early start."

"Yes, sir."

"It's just Clint."

"Yes, si—Clint. I'll be up early to get some breakfast into us before we go."

"That's good."

Wilkie walked away, and Clint tossed his bedroll under the wagon.

***

Wilkie found Lyle Peters standing by a wagon.

"He didn't find anything?" he asked.

"No," Peters said, "He didn't do that kind of a search."

The third man, who drove the wagon and claimed it as his, was Stu Barnard. He stood off to one side and waited. He was just a paid hand for the trip.

"So we're in the clear," Wilkie said.

"So far."

"Yeah," Barnard said, "but the Gunsmith. This don't sound smart to me."

"That's why you don't do the thinking, Stu," Peters said. "Without him, we wouldn't be getting this trip done."

"Okay," Barnard said, "whatever you say."

"Adams is bunking under the head wagon," Wilkie said. "I told him you'd be in your bedroll nearby."

"And I will be."

"I'll be closer to the wagon, so I can keep an eye on him."

"And you'll sleep here," Peters said to Barnard. "And don't let anybody near the wagon. Understand?"

"I got it," Barnard said.

"Adams wants to get an early start," Wilkie said, "but I told him I'd be up just as early to make breakfast."

"Okay, then," Peters said, "I'll see you in the morning."

Wilkie nodded and headed back to the head wagon.

"Is this gonna work?" Barnard asked Peters.

"I'm going to make damn sure it works," Peters said. "You just do what you're told."

"What about Horton?"

"Horton's just a scout," Peters said. "Don't worry about him."

"And Dave and Chuck?"

"They worked for the Major," Peters said, "they'll work for Adams."

"I'm still nervous about him bein' here," Barnard admitted, "but okay, I'm going along with ya."

"Good."

"What about the woman?"

"Don't worry about her," Peters said. "She knows what her job is."

"Okay, then I might as well turn in."

"Sleep inside the wagon," Peters said, "every night. Got it?"

"I've got it."

Lyle Peters nodded, turned and headed for his bedroll.

***

Clint went to check on Eclipse, who seemed to have been taken good care of by Mike Rowland. The other horses were standing relaxed, and Clint thought they were taking their cue from his big Darley.

"Okay, big boy," Clint said, "tomorrow we start a long trip

Eclipse nodded his head, and Clint stroked his big neck, then walked back to camp where the fire was still burning. Wilkie had left a pot of coffee there, and Clint poured himself a cup.

"Mind if I join you?"

He turned, saw Liz Landers standing there.

"Sure," Clint said. "Coffee?"

"Please."

She came into the camp, accepted a cup from him, and then they sat by the fire.

"Will we be leavin' tomorrow, as planned?" she asked.

"In the morning, after breakfast," Clint said.

"Are we makin' our own breakfasts?"

"Yes," Clint said. "There'll be times when we have a communal meal, but not tomorrow."

"Okay."

She sipped her coffee and stared out into the open.

"Are you all right?" he asked.

"I guess I'm nervous," she said. "I've never been on a trek like this."

"Liz, how long have you been alone?"

"My husband died three years ago," she said. "I've been alone since then. I don't make friends easily, and when I joined this wagon train, I just bonded with Delilah."

"So you'll be all right?"

"I'll be fine." She put the cup down and stood up. "I just wanted to take a walk before turning in, and I ended up here. I want to tell you, I feel safe with you in charge."

"I hope you feel that way from here to Reno, Liz," he said. "Would you like me to walk you back to your wagon?"

"No, that's not necessary," she said. "I'll be fine. Good-night, Clint."

He watched her walk away, along the line of wagons that stretched out into the night. There was a fire here and there, but for the most part people had turned in.

There was still coffee in the pot, so he left it on the fire, in case Wilkie, Peters or he wanted some during the night. Wilkie could empty it out in the morning and make it fresh.

He unrolled his bedroll beneath the wagon and turned in.

Chapter Twenty-One

In the morning, Clint smelled fresh coffee and bacon, as he rolled out from beneath the wagon.

"Bacon?" he asked, approaching the fire.

"And eggs," Wilkie said. "Almost ready. Here." He handed Clint a cup of coffee.

The second wagon, right behind the one Clint had slept underneath, was Wilkie's chuckwagon. Clint had inspected the outside, but not the inside, so he was surprised that the man had eggs.

"Think the rest of those eggs will survive the trip?" Clint asked.

"I got them packed real careful in my wagon," Wilkie said. "They ain't even gonna crack."

Lyle Peters came walking over, smiling.

"I smelled the bacon," he said, "got me right up."

Wilkie handed him a cup.

"How did you sleep?" he asked Clint.

"Fine," Clint said. "I'm rested and ready. Are people getting themselves around?"

"Oh, yeah," Peters said. "They'll all be ready to go."

"And the folks who are staying behind?"

"Turns out to only be three wagons, and they've already pulled out of line."

Wilkie came over and handed them each a plate, and a fork. They both found places to sit, near the fire. Wilkie then got himself a plate and joined them.

"So, how many miles a day do we want to do?" Peters asked.

"If I remember correctly," Clint said, "the Major favored fifteen to twenty. We'll start there."

"That was with larger trains," Peters said. "We should be able to do better than that."

"Some of these wagons don't have the horsepower for more," Clint said. "We'll have to see how their teams do in the beginning. Maybe later we can increase our rate."

"You've given this some thought," Peters said.

"Yes, I have," Clint said. "I'm not just a Wagonmaster in name only. If I'm going to do the job, I'm going to do it my way. I told you that from the beginning."

"Yes, you did."

"Then don't be surprised when I make a decision."

"I won't be," Peters said. He stood up. "Well, as Captain, it's my job to make sure everybody's ready to go, so I'll get to it."

As he started off, Bob Horton passed him coming the other way.

"Breakfast ready?" he asked.

"I'll get you a plate," Wilkie said.

"In the future, Horton," Clint said, "be here for break-fast when everybody else is. If you're not, you'll miss out. We won't be waiting."

Horton accepted a plate from Wilkie and said to Clint, "I'll keep that in mind."

"And I'll need you to get moving before the rest of us do," Clint added.

"What for? It's not like we have tribes of Indians to worry about. Those days are gone."

"You don't know what you have to worry about," Clint said. "That's why I want you out there with your eyes open, looking for trouble, whether it be Indians or a rock slide."

"Yes, sir!" Horton snapped. "I'll get right on that, sir."

"Finish your breakfast," Clint said, standing, "but keep in mind what I said."

Clint went to collect his bedroll, and decided to go and saddle Eclipse himself, instead of letting Mike Rowland do it. It was time to go. He could hear Major Tom Wallace in his head, yelling, "Wagon's Ho!"

Chapter Twenty-Two

The first day was uneventful.

According to Clint's calculations, they had covered about seventeen miles.

Horton rode well up ahead of them, Peters drove the head wagon while Wilkie drove his chuckwagon. Both of them had fine, solid teams.

Clint spent time riding up and down the line of wagons, examining each individual team and wagon. He spent time keeping a close eye on the wagons where the axles and wheels had been repaired, and they all seemed to be holding up well.

At one point, in the afternoon, he was riding alongside Delilah's wagon.

"How are you doing?" she asked.

"Fine," he said. "Looks like everybody's wagons are holding up, but we really haven't come to any rough terrain, yet."

"No," she said, "I meant, how are *you* doing?"

"Oh . . . well, I'm fine. I'm committed to this trip, now, so I'm not having any second thoughts."

"That's good. But shouldn't you be riding up front, and not back here?"

"I probably should," he said. "I'll check on you later."

"Fine."

Clint headed back to the front of the column, exchanging a wave with Liz Landers along the way.

***

They didn't stop for lunch, and never would. They'd continue on until they camped for the night, and then everyone could prepare their suppers.

Clint preferred not to stop the wagons in a circle, but to rather leave them in line. It would make for a quicker getaway each morning.

The first night they stopped as dusk fell, and Wilkie built his fire next to his wagon rather than the head wagon. He made another pot of stew that night, and Clint had a feeling they were going to be eating lots of stew on this trip.

Horton came riding back in as Wilkie was dishing the stew out. As he dismounted, Wilkie handed him a plate.

"Thanks."

"What's going on up ahead?" Clint asked.

"Nothin'," Horton said. "Flat ground for as far as I could go. We won't have any trouble for days."

"No Indians?" Wilkie asked.

"Not a one," Horton said. "If we do run into any, they should be small parties who left the reservation. They'll probably just want to trade."

"What about regular white bandits?" Wilkie asked. "They might get tired of robbing stagecoaches and trains and try for something slower moving."

"That's what Mr. Horton is going to be out there looking for, trouble," Clint said.

"You know," Horton said, "not finding anythin' out there makes it kind of lonely."

"We'll be passing a lot of populated areas," Clint said, "unlike the old days, when the wagon trains were covering virgin territory."

"I've got to wash up," Horton said, putting his empty plate down. "Should've done it before I ate, but I was too hungry."

He went off to wash in a barrel they kept strapped to the side of the wagon for that purpose.

"I gotta clean up," Wilkie said.

"I'm going to walk the train, check in with people, make sure everybody's okay," Clint said.

"Okay," Wilkie said. "I'll have some more coffee goin' when you get back."

"Great. Thanks."

Clint started walking.

***

Stu Barnard was just cleaning up after his supper when Clint Adams came walking up to his wagon.

"Just checking," Clint said, "to be sure everyone's equipment survived the first day. You are?"

"Stu Barnard."

"Right, right," Clint said. "Everything okay?"

"Everything's fine. Mr. Adams."

"Just call me Clint."

"The Major always wanted everyone to call him 'the Major.'"

"Well," Clint said, "I don't have any rank, so we won't have a problem."

"No sir," Barnard said. "I mean . . . Clint."

"Didn't mean to interrupt you," Clint said. "Go ahead with your cleaning."

"Thank you, si—Clint."

Clint moved on to the next wagon.

Barnard breathed a sigh of relief. He just wasn't comfortable around Clint Adams. Not when the man could kill him in the blink of an eye.

Those kind of men always intimidated him.

Chapter Twenty-Three

As Clint walked the length of the train, he saw camp-fires being built, some wagons preparing communal meals, others being more individual, and still others having already eaten. When he got to the next to last wagon, Liz Landers was starting her fire.

"Eating alone?" he asked.

"Unless you want to join me," she said, standing up. The dress she was wearing that day was a bit more form fitting. He could now see the body that had only been hinted at before.

"I've already eaten," he said. "Wilkie gets to his job quickly."

"I know," she said, "I'm only just gettin' started."

"What about Delilah?" he asked. "Don't you two eat together?"

"Sometimes we do," she said, "but not tonight."

"How was your first day?" he asked.

"It went fine," she said. "My team was steady, and my wagon very solid."

"That's good to hear. I'll go and check on Delilah's progress, now."

"If you change your mind about eatin' somethin', let me know," she said. "I'll always be available."

"I'll keep that in mind."

***

After Clint left to walk the train, Peters and Wilkie converged.

"First day went okay," Peters said. "How was the wagon?"

"Solid," Wilkie said, "but we knew we weren't gonna have to go over rough ground—not yet, anyway."

"Adams is pretty active," Peters said, "riding back and forth all day."

"I was prepared to have the Major on the wagon with me, but I just as soon not have Adams," Wilkie said.

"I've got to go check with Barnard."

"Go ahead," Wilkie said. "I'll clean up here and make some more coffee."

"Good idea," Peters said. "Keep Adams happy with that strong coffee of yours."

"Will do."

Peters left the camp to go to Stu Barnard's wagon and ask the same questions.

***

When Clint reached Delilah's wagon, she looked up from her fire in surprise.

"Well," she said, "I didn't think you'd get past Liz's wagon."

"And why's that?" he asked.

She giggled.

"We talked about you," she said. "I'm afraid I sang your praises."

"Oh, I see," he said. "Well, I'm going to be a little busy this whole trip."

"Hey," she said, "everybody goes to sleep eventually."

"Well, I'm just checking on your team and your wagon," he said. "How'd they do?"

"Just fine," she said, "we're all just fine. How bad can it get after only one day?"

"I know," Clint said. "We'll see how things go in the days to come."

"Coffee before you go?" she asked.

She was wearing trail clothes—boots, jeans and a man's shirt with the top three buttons undone to show her silky cleavage.

"I don't think so, Delilah," he said. "Not tonight anyway."

As he walked away, she muttered, "Scaredy-cat."

***

As Clint passed Stu Barnard's wagon, he saw the man standing with Lyle Peters, their heads close together. He wondered if Peters was just doing some of his Captain's duties, or if the two men had something else going?

He changed direction so that he passed the wagon without the two men seeing him. When he got back to the front wagon, Wilkie was poking at the fire with a long branch.

"Fresh coffee," he announced, when he saw Clint approaching.

"I smelled it."

Wilkie poured a cup, then said, "Sweetener?"

"No," Clint said, "just the coffee, thanks."

The cook handed it to him.

"I gotta go inside my wagon for a while," Wilkie said. "Plannin' meals, you know."

Clint wondered what kind of a stew the man would come up with tomorrow night.

Chapter Twenty-Four

Clint pretty much decided to follow the California Trail, which would take them from Missouri to Nebraska, to Wyoming, Utah, and then Nevada.

The first stop to restock was three weeks later, at Ft. Kearny, Nebraska. To that point there had been no shortage of supplies, only two breakdowns that had to be addressed and repaired, and he had managed to avoid the advances of both Liz and Delilah, who kept trying to get him into the back of their wagons.

Normally, he would not avoid two such willing women, but felt it was necessary, in order to keep the respect of everyone on board. The Wagonmaster certainly couldn't be seen sneaking in and out of ladies' wagons.

And it wasn't only Liz and Delilah who were interested. He could feel the eyes of both Ada Stevens and her daughter, Ellie, following him when he walked or rode by.

"Who's ridin' into Kearny for supplies?" Wilkie asked him.

"Well, I figure you and me," Clint said. "You're the only one who knows what you need for the chuckwagon."

"Fine with me," Wilkie said. "I could use a trip to town."

While they were hitching a horse to a buckboard for Wilkie, and saddling Eclipse, Liz Landers came along, wearing riding clothes.

"I've talked with some of the women on the train and we all need things from the mercantile. I thought I'd come along."

Clint and Wilkie exchanged a look.

"There's room on the buckboard," Wilkie said, with a shrug.

"I can ride," Liz said.

"I meant room for supplies," Wilkie said.

"Oh, okay, but I can ride," Liz repeated.

"Fine," Clint said.

He called Mike Rowland over and had him saddle a horse for Liz.

When he walked the horse over and handed the reins to Liz, they mounted up while Wilkie climbed up on the buckboard seat. Then the three of them headed for town.

***

When they reached town, Wilkie directed the buckboard right to the mercantile and stopped in front.

"I'm gonna load the buckboard and then go have a beer in a saloon," he said.

"Fine with me," Clint said, "I'm going to stick with the buckboard and make sure nothing gets stolen."

"I just have a few purchases," Liz said, dismounting. "Some of the women needed sewing supplies, and bolts of material."

Clint remained outside with the buckboard, and soon enough Wilkie and a clerk wearing a white apron started carrying supplies out and dumping them on the buckboard. While that was going on, Liz came out carrying some brown paper-wrapped bundles and a bag. Clint took them from her and set them down on the buckboard.

Wilkie came out carrying his last sack and dumped it on the buckboard.

"There's a saloon down the street according to the clerk," Wilkie said. "We in a hurry?"

"I just want to get back to camp before dark," Clint replied.

"No problem," Wilkie said. "I'll see you right here in a little while."

"Enjoy," Clint said.

"Don't you want to go for a beer?" Liz asked him.

"No," Clint said, "the last time somebody from the train went shopping, I had to stop some jaspers from stealing." He waved at the buckboard. "This looks too easy."

"Well, I asked the clerk if we could pull the buckboard around back, and he said there's a big empty space out there. We just have to turn down this street, then take an alley. He says nobody ever goes back there. Then we could go and get a cup of coffee somewhere."

"Okay," Clint said, not seeing any harm in that, "let's go."

He helped Liz up on the buckboard seat, then tied the two horses to the back and joined her. Following the directions from the clerk, he drove the buckboard around to the back of the mercantile and saw what he meant. There was no reason for anyone to go back there. It was a large area, though, with plenty of room for them to turn around when they left.

"This is good," he said. "I'm glad you asked."

"So am I," she said.

He got down, helped her down, and started back up the alley.

"Wait a minute, Clint," she said. "I have to get something from the back."

"Go ahead."

He waited by the front of the buckboard, heard her moving around in the back.

"Clint?" she called. "Can you help me?"

"Sure."

He walked to the back of the buckboard, turned, and saw her lying on top of some of the sacks Wilkie had loaded.

She was naked.

Chapter Twenty-Five

"Liz—" he said, but stopped short when she pushed herself up onto one arm.

The body that had been hinted at was now on full display. She had small but firm breasts, like ripe peaches, and otherwise was a slender, yet strong woman. He could see the muscles in her arms and legs as she posed for him. And between her legs was a wild patch as black as the hair on her head.

"You've been avoiding me during the trip," she said.

"It wouldn't do for me to be seen sneaking in and out of your wagon," he said. "Or Delilah's."

"Well, now you don't have to sneak," she said. "We have this area all to ourselves."

"Right out in the open?" he asked.

"Don't be a chicken, Mr. Gunsmith," she said. "Climb up here and mount me. I've waited long enough."

Clint looked around, saw that they were quite alone, with no windows anywhere nearby.

"What about Delilah?" he asked. "What are we going to tell her?"

"Delilah has already agreed to share," Liz said, with a sexy smile. "After all, we're friends."

She crooked a finger at him.

"Come on, stop wastin' time," she said. "We don't want Mr. Wilkie to come lookin' for us."

He *had* been finding it difficult to resist both women during the first three weeks of the trip, and now here was one of them offering to solve that problem—at least for now.

"Damn you, woman!" he said, climbing up on the buckboard with her.

It was a warm day, but he could feel the heat from her body as he got closer to her. He took off his gunbelt and set it aside, and then allowed her to help him off with his clothes. He didn't bother removing his boots, because this was going to be fast. She wanted him to mount her, and that's just what he intended to do. There was no time for anything else.

By the time he crouched between her thighs, he was already hard. He could also smell that she was ready. Just for a moment, he put his hand on her crotch, felt her heat and wetness, and then pressed the head of his cock to her vagina and pushed.

"Oh yrahhhhh," she breathed as he drove into her. "Yessssss." She wrapped her legs around his waist.

He began to pound in and out of her, and neither of them was concerned, anymore, about someone coming along.

The sacks shifted beneath their weight, but they managed to stay linked as he pounded away causing her to grunt in between her comments describing how good it was.

"Uhhhh . . . oh damn, this is . . . uhhhhn . . . so good . . . keep going . . . ooooh . . . faster . . ."

The buckboard actually began to rock from side-to-side, causing the horses to shift about, but, luckily, did not spook them. It would have been very embarrassing for a horse to panic and run out into the middle of the street, with Clint and Liz naked on the back of the buckboard.

Clint began to move faster and faster as he felt his release building up in his legs, coming up his thighs and then suddenly erupting inside of her. Just before that, beating him to her finish, Liz's body began to tremble and then she started to buck. He exploded while she was still in the throes of her pleasure, so they had almost managed to reach their release at the same time . . .

***

Clint dressed quickly, now suddenly concerned that someone might come walking along.

"Relax," Liz said, pulling on her shirt. "I told you, the clerk said nobody ever comes back here."

"And what if he was out here?" Clint asked. "There's a window on the back wall, probably a storeroom. What if he snuck back there to watch?"

"Why would he?" she asked. "I didn't tell him why I was bringin' you here?"

"What if he figured it out?"

"Then he got an eyeful," she said, buttoning her shirt. "So what?"

Liz had even taken the time to remove her boots, so now she sat on the edge of the buckboard to pull them back on.

Clint had done his deed with his boots still on, and his pants bunched around his ankles. Not the most comfortable way to have sex, but he soon forgot about it.

When they were both fully dressed and Clint had his gun on, they climbed up onto the buckboard seat and drove back around to the front of the mercantile. No sooner had Clint applied the brake, Wilkie came along, crossing over from the other side of the street.

Clint got down and helped Liz down.

"What were you two doin'?" Wilkie asked, climbing up into the seat.

"Nothing much. Just sitting and waiting for you," Clint said.

Chapter Twenty-Six

When they got back to the train, Liz Landers returned to her wagon with her packages, while Clint, Wilkie and a couple of others unloaded the supplies and put them in Wilkie's chuckwagon.

"Anything happen in town?" Peters asked.

"Nothin' to me," Wilkie said. "I don't know about those two."

Peters looked at Clint, since Liz was already gone.

"Nothing with us," he said. "We just stayed with the buckboard."

"I got to get supper started," Wilkie said, and went to the fire.

"So we're set to continue?" Peters asked Clint.

"As far as I'm concerned, yeah," Clint said. "I don't think we'll have to stop for supplies again until Fort Laramie."

"That's good to hear," Peters said. "Some of the folks were asking me."

"Well, you tell them we don't expect any difficulties in the near future."

"Right. I'll tell 'em."

Clint nodded, went to the barrel attached to the side of the chuckwagon to wash up.

***

When Liz came out of her wagon after storing only her purchases—since she really hadn't talked with any other women before going—Delilah came along.

"Well?"

"You're right," she said. "He's a beautiful man, but I really didn't have the time to get a closer look." She took a deep breath and then let it out. "He just *took* me."

"You dirty bitch!" Delilah said, and they both laughed. "Tell me all about it!"

***

Clint accepted the plate from Wilkie and sat by the fire.

"Not stew?" Clint asked.

"I managed to get a few chickens in town," Wilkie said. "Just enjoy."

Peters came along and accepted a plate.

"Looks like everybody came through the first three weeks okay," he said. "And, believe it or not, nobody's complaining."

"That's good," Clint said. "So's this," he added, tapping his plate with his fork.

"Thanks," Wilkie said. "I know I'm the stew king, but I thought you might want somethin' different."

"Once in a while," Clint said, "something different is nice."

"I'll do my best," Wilkie said. "I should be able to do it with some of the supplies I bought today. Also, if somebody would go huntin' . . ."

"I'll keep that in mind," Clint said. "Maybe we have some experienced hunters along. Or maybe Horton can bring something back with him. By the way, where is Horton? He usually eats with us."

"I don't know," Peters said. "Maybe he got invited by somebody else."

"He doesn't have a woman on the train, does he?"

"He wishes," Wilkie said, laughing.

"He doesn't," Peters said, "unless Delilah Rogers has suddenly given in to his charms. Which I doubt."

Clint passed his empty plate to Wilkie.

"More?" the cook asked.

"Maybe when I get back."

"Where are you going?" Peters asked.

"I want to find Horton," Clint said. "Talk to him about hunting."

Clint left the camp.

"What do you think that's about?" Wilkie asked.

J.R. Roberts

"I don't know," Peters said. "He might just be assert-
ing his authority."

"Horton's not gonna like that," Wilkie said.

Peters shrugged and kept eating.

***

Clint walked the length of the train without locating
Bob Horton. When he got to Liz's wagon, she wasn't
there. When he reached Delilah's, she and Liz were
sitting around a fire, eating and laughing.

"What's so funny?" he asked.

They both looked up at him, and then Delilah said,
"Just girl talk. What's wrong?"

"Have either of you seen Horton?"

"I haven't," Liz said.

"No." Delilah said.

"Has he been . . . bothering either of you?"

"Not me," Liz said, "but he's stuck on Delilah."

"Liz!"

"Well, he is," Liz said.

"Have you encouraged him, at any time?" Clint asked.

"No," she said, firmly.

"Why not? Isn't he a good-looking guy?"

"Until he speaks," Liz said.

"Then his personality comes out," Delilah said.

"I get it," Clint said. He'd known quite a few attractive women who were less attractive once you got to know them. And then there were the less attractive people who got more attractive the longer you knew them. There was more to people than just the way they looked.

"Okay," he said, "you can go back to your girl talk."

As he walked away, he heard them laughing again, and couldn't help wondering if they were talking about him.

***

"Do you think he knows we were talkin' about him?" Liz asked.

"He's a smart man," Delilah said. "He can figure it out."

"Why didn't you tell him about you and Horton?"

"Because it was one time and never happened again," Delilah said, "and never will. I just had an itch I needed to scratch."

"And Horton did it?"

Delilah rolled her eyes and said, "Just barely."

Chapter Twenty-Seven

When Clint got back to the front wagon, Horton was there, sitting at the fire eating.

"Where've you been?" Clint asked.

"Doin' my job," Horton said. "Havin' a look around the area to be sure we're safe."

"And?"

"It looks clear," Horton said.

Clint thought it would. So far, in three weeks, there had been none of the hardships wagon trains of twenty or thirty years ago were forced to endure. The trip had been smooth, even though for some of it they were following the ruts permanently dug into the ground by those bygone trains.

Wilkie handed Clint a cup of coffee.

"Thanks." He looked around. "Now where's Peters?"

"He's the Captain," Wilkie said. "He's off doin' Captain duties."

Clint realized that he had probably been doing some of the things Peters thought were his job, but he felt he was just being thorough.

Clint sat at the fire, drinking his coffee and stared out into the darkness.

***

From some distance away, a group of men were sitting on their horses, looking at the many fires that were burning next to the wagons.

"When are we gonna do this?" Gene Shelton asked.

"When Horton says so," Buck Gentry said. "It's his play, after all."

Shelton turned and looked at the other four men, who were sitting quietly.

"I don't have the patience the rest of you do," he said. "And I don't know Horton that well."

"Well, I do," Gentry said. "Don't worry about it, Shelton. He'll tell us when the time comes."

"Look at them," Shelton said. "They're all sittin' ducks, right now. Why don't we just ride on in—"

"Relax," Gentry said.

"I was just thinkin'—"

"Stop thinkin'," Gentry said. "That ain't what you're gettin' paid for. We got plenty of time before this train gets where it's goin'. Horton is gonna pick just the right time and place. And it may not be for a while."

"That's what I'm afraid of."

***

Clint walked over to where the horses were picketed, saw Mike Rowland standing by Eclipse, brushing him.

"Checkin' up on us?" he asked.

"Checking on him," Clint said. "I realize you know what you're doing."

"I appreciate that."

"How are the rest?" Clint asked.

"They all seem sound, and they're standin' quiet."

"And Eclipse?"

"Not so quiet," Rowland admitted. "I'm brushing him because he was fidgety."

"That usually means something."

"Like what?"

"Like maybe he knows something we don't," Clint said, staring out into the dark.

"Like what?" Rowland asked again.

"I guess we'll find out, sooner or later," Clint said.

Chapter Twenty-Eight

The next three weeks also went fairly smoothly, as they moved through Nebraska to Wyoming, and headed for Fort Laramie.

In the evenings, Eclipse was still somewhat fidgety, causing Clint to think that somebody might be following them, keeping an eye on them for some reason. They certainly hadn't made a move yet, and had not even come close enough for him to see them.

As they made camp outside of Fort Laramie, Wilkie looked at Clint and said, "What do you keep lookin' for?"

"I don't know," Clint said, staring out over the plains. "Something."

"What about Horton?" Wilkie said. "He don't seem to feel there's anythin' to worry about."

"I know," Clint said. "That's what worries me."

"Well," Wilkie said, "then send 'im out to do his job."

"I might do that," Clint said. He looked at Wilkie. "What's for supper?"

"Stew," the cook said, "but I'm doin' somethin' different to it."

"Good."

"We goin' into Fort Laramie tomorrow?" Wilkie said. "I could use some supplies, and a beer."

"Yeah, why not?" Clint said.

Wilkie went back to his stew pot, and Clint went back to his staring.

***

"I'm a nervous wreck," Stu Barnard said to Lyle Peters.

"Well, don't be," Peters said. "Jesus, all you've got to do is drive this wagon. Any decisions that need to be made will be made by me."

"Adams comes by here every night," the man complained.

"I know he does," Peters said, "but he walks by all the wagons every night, so don't worry about it."

"Why does he do that?" Barnard asked. "Ain't that your job?"

"He's just trying to let the people know he's here," Peters said. "And not in name only."

"Still—"

"Stop worrying!" Peters finally snapped, impatiently. "Everything is going fine."

"How about lettin' me ride into Fort Laramie tomorrow?" Barnard asked.

"What for?"

"Just to get a beer," Barnard said.

"You know what?" Peters said. "I'll ask the Wagon-master."

"Wha—" Barnard started, but Peters walked away.

***

Clint walked the wagons again that night, stopped to talk to several of the families, as he had started doing. Some of them would offer him a drink, or coffee, or even food. Sometimes he said yes, sometimes no. On this night, the Stevens family was sitting around their fire as he approached their wagon.

"Clint!" Ellie said, smiling happily. "I—we've been waiting for you."

"Have you?"

Clearly, Abraham Stevens hadn't been waiting for him, because the man did not look happy.

"Something to eat, Clint?" Ada asked.

"Not tonight, Ada," Clint said. "Wilkie tells me he's done something new with his stew."

"We should have a communal meal tomorrow night," Ada said. "We haven't done that yet."

"That sounds good to me, Ada."

"Young Jerry Reed, from the next wagon, plays the mouth harp. And I think Auggie Davis plays guitar. We could have some music."

"Let's see what happens tomorrow," Clint said. "Wilkie and I are going to town for some supplies. We'll see what time we get back."

"I can make the arrangements," Ada offered.

"I might take you up on that."

"Let the man do his job," Abraham said.

"He's right, I have to keep walking."

"Can I walk with you a bit?" Ellie asked.

"Sure," Clint said, "if it's okay with your mother."

"Oh, she doesn't mind!" Ellie said, and linked her arm in his.

"Let's go, then," he said.

They walked on, with Ellie chattering away, but holding on tightly to his left arm.

***

When Clint and Ellie approached Delilah's wagon, she and Liz were sitting at her fire, and spotted them.

"Look at that little hussy, hangin' onto him," Liz said.

"She's a baby, Liz," Delilah said. "Nothin' to worry about."

"She's a pretty thing," Liz said.

"Clint likes women," Delilah said. "I think he's already proved that."

They both put smiles on as Clint and Ellie approached.

Chapter Twenty-Nine

"Hello, ladies," Clint said.

"Clint," Liz said.

"Hello, Ellie," Delilah said.

"Hello Miss Rogers, Miss Landers," Ellie said. "I just thought I'd keep Clint company on his walk tonight."

"Well, how nice," Liz said.

"Would either of you like some coffee?" Delilah asked.

"No, thanks," Clint said. "Wilkie's waiting supper for me."

"Not for me, thank you," Ellie said. "But I want to tell you ladies, we might be having a communal meal tomorrow night. With music."

"Well," Delilah said, "that sounds interesting."

"When will we know for sure?" Liz asked.

"When Wilkie and I get back from Fort Laramie," Clint said.

"Oh, you're goin' into town?" Liz said, perking up. "Maybe I'll come along—"

"We're going to make a quick trip," Clint said, cutting her off, "grab some supplies, and get back. I don't think you'll have time to shop."

"Oh," Liz said, "well, that was what I was thinkin' of doin'. . . shop."

"Next time," Clint said. "Good-night, ladies. I'll just walk Ellie back to her parent's wagon and go have my supper."

"Enjoy it, Clint."

Clint nodded, as he and Ellie walked off.

"You're a bold bitch," Delilah said to Liz, with a smile.

"Look who's talkin'," Liz said, smiling back.

***

"Those two ladies like you, Clint," Ellie said, as they walked back.

"Really?"

"Come on," she said, tugging on his arm, "you know they do. And you know I do."

"Ellie—"

"Momma does, too," she said, giggling. "It makes Pa mad."

"Well, I don't want to make your father mad."

"Oh," Ellie said, "my Pa doesn't need to know what we do. Would you like to kiss me?"

"Ellie," Clint said, "you're very pretty, but you're also very young."

"I know how to kiss," she assured him.

"I'm sure you do," he said. "And I'm sure there are some boys on this wagon train who would like to kiss you."

"But not you?"

"I'm not a boy," he said.

"So, you'd rather kiss Momma?"

"Your mother is a married woman," Clint said. "Kissing her would really make your Pa mad, wouldn't it?"

"It sure would," she said, then giggled and added, "but it might make him appreciate her more."

"I'm afraid you'll have to find a way to make him do that without using me."

***

Clint left Ellie back at her parent's wagon and continued on.

"Yer just in time," Wilkie said. "Here ya go." He handed Clint a plate of stew.

"Thanks."

Peters and Horton were also there, so they all sat around the fire with their plates and cups.

"Wilkie wants to go to town for supplies tomorrow," Clint said, "so I thought I'd go with him."

"Suits me," Peters said.

"I don't care," Horton said. "I'll be ridin' out tomorrow to take a look around."

"Good," Clint said, "then we all know what we'll be doing. But Ada and Ellie Stevens asked if we could do a communal meal tomorrow night."

"With who cookin'?" Wilkie asked.

"I assume everybody'll bring something," Clint said. "And they want to have music."

"The Reed kid's mouth organ?" Peters asked.

"And somebody else's guitar."

Peters shrugged.

"Sounds okay to me," he said. "I can get together with them while you fellas are in town and set it up."

"You do that," Clint said. "We won't be getting back from town late."

"Sounds like a good celebration for our first six weeks," Peters said.

"Agreed," Clint said. He looked at Wilkie. "Is there bacon in this stew?"

***

Before turning in, Clint walked over to the horses, as he did each night. As usual, Rowland was paying special attention to Eclipse.

"Same tonight?" he asked.

"Yep," Rowland said, "fidgety."

"Well," Clint said, "whoever's out there, I wish they'd make their move."

"You think they're gonna hit us?"

"Just keep your rifle ready," Clint said.

"I always do."

Rowland had his own wagon, but Clint had no idea when or where the man ate.

Clint stroked Eclipse's neck, then turned and walked back toward the fire. When he got there, Horton and Peters were gone, and Wilkie was sitting alone.

"What's going on, Wilkie?"

"Huh?"

"Horton and Peters, they seem to both have their own agenda."

Wilkie stared at Clint, then said, "I don't know what that means. Agenda?"

Clint had already come to the conclusion that the cook was smarter than he let on.

"Maybe," he said, "I don't know what I mean, either."

Chapter Thirty

In the morning Wilkie got his buckboard ready while Clint saddled Eclipse. He was having second thoughts about going into town, wondering if whoever was watching them would choose today to hit. In the end, though, he didn't think they would. They were apparently waiting for just the right time and place, and Clint didn't think this was it. They were too close to the law in Fort Laramie. When they did hit, it was going to be out in the middle of nowhere—perhaps between Fort Laramie and Salt Lake City.

He rode Eclipse over to where Wilkie was climbing onto the seat of the buckboard.

"Ready?" he asked.

"As I'll ever be."

Clint looked down at Peters.

"Like I said, we'll be back early."

"Don't worry," Peters said, "I'll have everything under control."

"I know you will," Clint said.

They started off with Clint riding right next to the buckboard.

***

J.R. Roberts

"That's Adams," Gene Shelton said. "Ridin' next to the cook."

"So?" Buck Gentry said.

"With him out of camp, the pickin' would be easy," Shelton said.

"We ain't here for pickin's, Gene," Gentry said. "We're here for a particular . . . pickin'."

"Well, all we been doin' for six weeks is ridin'," Shelton said.

"Gene," Gentry said, "nobody else is gettin' antsy. Why are you?"

"Maybe you guys have forever to waste," Shelton said, "I don't."

"Then I suggest you pull out," Gentry said. "The five of us can get this done."

"Oh sure, then you get my split," Shelton said. "No way. I'm stayin'."

"Then settle down and wait for the word to come," Gentry said.

***

Clint and Wilkie rode into Fort Laramie at what looked like a peak time. People were on the boardwalks, horses and wagons were on the street.

"This is a lively lookin' place," Wilkie said.

"We're only three hours from Denver," Clint said. "There's got to be some overflow."

"There's a general store," Wilkie said. "I'm goin' there. Where you goin'?"

"I'll stick with you," Clint said. "I can help you load the wagon."

"And then a beer?" Wilkie asked.

"And then one beer," Clint agreed.

"Okay."

Wilkie directed the horse pulling the buckboard over to the general store, reined the animal in right in front. Clint dismounted, just looped Eclipse's reins loosely over a nearby hitching post.

Wilkie started for the door, then turned and looked at Clint.

"You comin'?"

"I thought I'd wait out here," Clint said. "Let me know when you're done, and I'll help you carry the stuff out."

Wilkie nodded, waved and went inside.

Chapter Thirty-One

Clint's goal, by remaining outside the store with Eclipse and the buckboard, was to keep an eye out and see if anyone was particularly interested in them. Eclipse's fidgety attitude for weeks convinced him that someone was trailing the wagon train, waiting for a chance to hit it. Maybe that someone had also followed them to town.

No matter where he looked, though, no one seemed concerned about them. Fort Laramie was a busy town, and people were busy with their own business.

But while he was standing there, leaning against the buckboard, a man approached, the sun glinting off the badge on his chest.

"'mornin'," the man greeted.

"Sheriff."

"You with the wagon train outside of town?"

"I am," Clint said. "I'm the Wagonmaster."

"Don't see many wagon trains on the old California Trail, anymore," the lawman said.

"So I understand."

"You wouldn't be bringin' any of your folks into town, wouldja?"

"Nope," Clint said. "We're just here overnight, to pick up supplies. We'll be heading out again tomorrow morning."

"Well that's good. My name's Sheriff Morgan, in case you need anythin' while you're here."

"I appreciate that."

The sheriff squinted at him.

"You got a name?"

Clint knew the man's attitude was going to change when he learned his name, but he didn't usually lie when asked.

"The name's Clint Adams."

He saw the name register, just a slight stiffening on the lawman's part.

"I never heard about the Gunsmith turning Wagonmaster," he finally commented.

"It's a one-time thing," Clint said. "A favor for an old friend."

"Uh-huh," Sheriff Morgan said. "You waitin' here for anythin' special?"

"My cook's inside picking up the supplies," Clint said. "I'm going to help him load the buckboard, then buy him a beer and head back."

"Not what you'd usually find a Wagonmaster doin'," Morgan said. He appeared to be in his fifties, had probably seen a good number of Wagonmasters in his time.

"Like I said," Clint repeated, "I'm just doin' this as a favor for a friend."

"A lot of time to donate to a favor," Morgan said.

"Sheriff," Clint said, "is there some reason in particular you came over here?"

"I usually like to check up on strangers in town, before they get into any kind of trouble," Morgan said. "Now that I know who you are—"

"I'm not here looking for trouble, Sheriff. Like I said, some supplies, a beer, and then back to our camp. We'll be gone by morning."

"Okay, Mr. Adams," Morgan said, "I'll take you at your word."

"I appreciate that."

"Have a good trip, the rest of the way."

The sheriff sauntered away, trying a little too hard to seem relaxed, even though he'd been tense since he found out who Clint was.

Wilkie came out at that point.

"Who was that?" he asked.

"The local sheriff."

"What'd he want?"

"Just a few questions," Clint said. "Are you ready to load up?"

"Yup."

"Then let's get to it."

***

After the buckboard was loaded, they crossed the street to a saloon called The Hay Bale. It was noisy and busy, but they managed to elbow a couple of places at the bar and order two beers.

Once they had them, they started to drink when a man next to Wilkie jostled him, spilling some of his beer. It didn't manage to splash onto Wilkie himself, but rather the man who had bumped him.

"What the hell!" the man yelled. He turned to look at Wilkie, and to do that he had to look down. "Look what ya did, ya runt!"

"You bumped into me, Mister," Wilkie said, "and who you callin' a runt, ya big jackass."

The big ass had some friends with him, and now they crowded in behind and began jawing at Wilkie, who gave back as good as he got. Clint sipped his beer and watched, not expecting the confrontation to get physical. After all, it was just a few drops of beer.

But the four men gradually began to get more and more irate at Wilkie, so Clint finally tapped him on the shoulder.

"Drink up," he said. "We've got to go."

"Drink up? I ain't even had a chance to take a sip, thanks to this big lug."

"Who you callin' a lug?" the big man snapped.

"He didn't mean anything by it," Clint said. "We're just going to leave."

"I oughtta blow your fool head off!" the big man said to Wilkie.

"I ain't wearin' a gun," the cook said, "but if you wanna step outside, I'll give ya a whippin', man-to-man."

The big man and his friends found that hysterical.

"If we go out into the street, I'll end up killin' ya," the big man said, "and then I'll hafta deal with the sheriff." He looked at Clint. "Why don't you give 'im your gun, and we'll settle this right here."

"And if you shoot him," Clint asked, "you won't get in trouble with the sheriff?"

"Nah," the man said, "Morgan just don't want me beatin' any more men to death. But he won't argue with a fair fight."

"This man's a cook," Clint said, "not a gun hand. What kind of fair fight is that?"

"I tell ya what," the man said. "I'll get him a gun from somebody else. You keep yours and stand with him. Then it'll be a fair fight."

"Ha!" Wilkie said. "You don't know what you're gettin' into, fella."

"Quiet," Clint said. "Us two against you, you call that fair?"

"Naw," the man said, "you two against us four. Now that's fair. You look like you know yer way around a gun,"

"You don't know the half of it," Wilkie said, finally taking a gulp of his beer. "I'm for that! Gimme a gun."

"Wilkie" Clint said, "shut up."

"Come on, Clint," Wilkie said, "you and me, we can take these four."

The situation was getting dangerously close to an explosion, and Clint didn't want to have to deal with the sheriff because he killed some drunks.

"You fellas shouldn't mess with these boys," the bartender said. "These are the Bassett boys."

"So?" Clint asked.

"Well, Lee Bassett, there, he's a big fella who likes to beat men down with his fists. But the others, they're his brothers, and they're all gun hands. They're always tryin' to suck strangers into a fight."

The Bassett boys were nudging each other and laughing, and then they all turned to face Clint and Wilkie. The big one, Lee Bassett, had a gun in his hands.

"Here ya go, shorty," Lee Bassett said.

Wilkie started to reach for the gun . . .

Chapter Thirty-Two

"Don't!" Clint snapped, and yanked Wilkie back away from the gun, spilling more of his beer.

"Aw, geez—" Wilkie said, as the beer splashed on him, this time.

Clint stepped between Lee Bassett and Wilkie and said, "There's not going to be any gunplay here."

Bassett grinned at Clint showing yellow teeth tinged with black from chewing tobacco.

"But my brothers love gunplay," he said. "Don'tcha boys?"

"We sure do," one of them said.

"This is my brother Dean," Lee said. "He's the fastest gun in Fort Laramie."

"Not no more, he ain't," Wilkie said. "This here's Clint Adams."

For some reason it had gotten quiet at that moment, "And Wilkie's voice seemed to fill the place as he yelled Clint's name.

"Jesus," somebody in the back said, "that feller's the Gunsmith."

"He ain't not," Lee Bassett said, staring at Clint. "You ain't the Gunsmith."

"He is, too," Wilkie said. "And he don't need me to take up a gun. He can handle the four of you all by hisself!"

"Lemme do it, Lee," Dean Bassett said. "I kin take 'im."

"If I let you get killed," Lee said, "I'd never hear the end of it."

"That's good thinking, Lee," Clint said. "Let's just forget this ever happened and I'll buy you four fellas a beer."

"Naw," Lee Bassett said, "I ain't gonna forget it. And I ain't gonna let Dean go up against you alone. All four of us is gonna kill ya."

"Lee—"

"Whether you're the Gunsmith or not," Lee Bassett went on. "If you ain't, too bad. If you are, we're gonna be the brothers who killed ya."

"Your sheriff is not going to like this," Clint said.

"He don't bother us none," Bassett said.

"No," Clint said, "I meant he's going to give me a hard time for killing the four of you."

The brothers laughed at that.

"You ain't gonna kill us," Dean Bassett said. "We're the Bassett Boys."

Chapter Thirty-Three

Wilkie moved away from the bar, but before he did, he grabbed Clint's almost full beer off the bar and took it with him.

Behind him, a man moved away from his friends and asked, "Is that really the Gunsmith?"

"It sure is," Wilkie said. "He's my Wagonmaster."

The man went back to his friends and said, "I got twenty on the Gunsmith."

There was a flurry of betting after that, and Wilkie turned and said, "I got two bucks on Clint."

"You're on," somebody said. "The Bassett Boys ain't never even got a scratch."

"They're gonna get worse than that," Wilkie said.

"You got more than two bucks?" a man asked.

"I got a whole buckboard full of supplies in front of the general store," Wilkie said. "You got fifty dollars?"

"You're covered," the man said.

Wilkie grinned and watched, drinking Clint's beer.

Clint saw that he didn't have a choice, so he started dividing the Bassett Boys. He didn't think he had to worry about Lee. The man was too big to properly handle a gun.

Dean seemed to have the bigger reputation in town, so he'd have to take him first. He didn't know the other two brothers' names, but he figured he'd find out after.

He wasn't going to have to explain this to the sheriff, because these boys weren't giving him a choice, there was betting going on, and this had happened before.

"You call it, Dean," Lee Bassett said. "You're the fastest."

Now Clint had a big advantage, because the brothers were going to wait for Dean to call it.

He wasn't.

He drew.

The Bassetts all looked shocked.

A gasp went up from the crowd of people who were watching from a safe distance.

Clint could have simply wounded the man, but there were too many of them. It was foolish to do anything but shoot to kill when you were facing multiple men. One of them could always get lucky and put a bullet in him, and he couldn't take that risk, especially with Dean Bassett.

So he shot Dean Bassett first, dead center in the chest. Despite the hunk of lead that punched him in the chest, he got his gun out, but when he pulled the trigger the gun was pointing at the floor.

The other two brothers were outclassed, never got their guns to clear leather before Clint shot them both in the chest.

And then came Lee Bassett. He was so big Clint couldn't help but hit him center mass.

All the Bassetts hit the floor. And Wilkie turned to accept his money.

***

When the sheriff walked in, he took one look at the fallen men, and Clint Adams, who by then had already ejected his spent shells and reloaded, just in case the Bassetts had some friends in the saloon.

"What the hell—" he said.

"They didn't give him no choice, Sheriff," the bartender said. "You know how them Bassett Boys is—was."

Morgan looked at Clint.

"You gunned the four of 'em?"

"Like the bartender said, Sheriff," Clint said. "They didn't give me any choice."

"What was the reason?" the lawman asked.

"Some spilled beer," Clint said.

"Jesus," Morgan said, shaking his head.

"They was after me, Sheriff," Wilkie said, stepping up to the bar. "Clint took my place. Or they woulda killed me."

Morgan looked at Clint.

"This is my cook, Mr. Wilkie."

"Everybody in here will tell ya," Wilkie said, "they didn't give him no choice."

"I don't need any more people to tell me that," Morgan said. "These boys have been pushin' for fights for a long time. They finally pushed the wrong person, I guess."

"I tried to talk them out of it."

"Are you ready to leave town, Adams?"

"We are, Sheriff."

"Then get goin'," Morgan said.

"These boys don't have any other brothers or cousins I'll have to worry about, do they?" Clint asked.

"No, they've got no family. Their Ma died last year. She was the last one."

Clint found comfort in that. He would have hated to be the man who had to tell their mother that all four of her sons were dead.

"Let's go, Wilkie."

Clint and the cook left the saloon and crossed the street to where they left the buckboard and Eclipse. On the way, Wilkie was counting his winnings.

J.R. Roberts

"What's that?"

"I bet on ya," Wilkie said.

"You what?"

"They was takin' bets," Wilkie said, "so I went ahead and bet."

"Bet what?"

"Well," Wilkie said, "I started with two dollars, which was all I had, but . . . I hadda bet more."

"Where did you get more?"

"I, uh, well . . . I bet the supplies."

They reached the buckboard and Clint turned to face the little cook.

"You did what?"

"I bet the supplies."

"How much did you win?"

"Well . . . I got fifty dollars from one feller, and then my two dollars . . . so I won fifty-two dollars."

"Give me the fifty," Clint said.

"What?"

"We'll put it in the kitty for the wagon train," Clint said. "You can keep the other two dollars you won."

"Aw geez—"

"I'm not letting you benefit from my having to kill four men," Clint said.

Wilkie reluctantly slapped the fifty dollars into Clint's hand.

"What's the difference?" he asked. "This can't be so different for you than any of the other men you killed over the years."

"And just how many men do you think I've killed?" Clint demanded.

"I dunno," Wilkie said. "Hundreds?"

"Jesus, Wilkie," Clint said, "do you believe everything you hear?"

"'kay, okay," Wilkie said, "dozens."

"Get up on that buckboard before I make you number five today," Clint growled.

Wilkie snapped his mouth shut and did as he was told. Clint walked over to Eclipse, mounted up and looked across the street. A crowd of men from the saloon had moved out onto the boardwalk to watch him. They were probably just making sure he was leaving town.

Clint thought about the Bassetts as they rode back to camp, and as they approached, he could hear the mouth organ and guitar music. After killing four men, he really didn't feel like a communal dinner, but he didn't have a choice.

Chapter Thirty-Four

Clint and Wilkie got Chuck and Dave to help them unload the buckboard, then Wilkie had to rush to get his food going. Many of the other women had brought offerings with them so there was plenty to go around.

As Clint joined the fray, people were dancing, and when Liz and Delilah saw him, they hurried over before young Ellie could get to him.

"You gotta dance with us," Liz said.

"I'm not much in the mood for dancing," Clint said.

"Somethin' happen in town?" Delilah asked.

"Yes," Clint said, "but I don't really want to talk about it."

"Suppose Wilkie wants to talk about it?" Liz asked.

"I'm sure he does."

The two women were smart enough to leave him alone—at least, for the moment—and hurried over to ask Wilkie their questions.

Lyle Peters came over, and had obviously already spoken with the cook.

"Rough time in town, I heard," he said.

"Pretty rough."

"That Wilkie," Peters said, "he'll get himself into trouble. He's lucky you were there."

"I wish I'd known that about him," Clint said. "I wouldn't have taken him to a saloon."

Clint saw Horton with young Ellie Stevens.

"I thought Horton was going to be out doing his job," Clint said.

"He was," Peters said. "According to him, there's nobody around to worry about."

"That's not what my horse says," Clint replied.

"What?"

"Never mind," Clint said. "Enjoy the party."

Clint called Chuck and Dave over, as well as Mike Rowland.

"Keep your rifles with you."

"Are we expectin' trouble?" Chuck asked.

"We're just going to be ready for anything," Clint said. "While everybody's eating and dancing would be a good time to hit us, don't you think?"

"Hit us?" Dave asked. "For what?"

"For whatever they can get," Clint said. "Just keep an eye out."

"Sure," Rowland said. "We can do that."

"And if you want to dance or eat," Clint said, "do it one at a time."

"Okay," Dave said, and the other two nodded their understanding.

With the three men out on alert, he went to get something to eat.

And dance.

Chapter Thirty-Five

It took the train almost forty-three days to get outside of Salt Lake City, when it should have taken thirty-three. Several wagons had broken down, two families had to be combined into one wagon, one family had to be separated from the train due to illness—then readmitted when the illness passed.

Also, six horses had been injured and put down. Horton managed to find a ranch nearby where they were able to buy several new animals.

One of the horses that needed to be put down was Horton's. His animal stepped in a chuck hole and snapped its leg. So they had to find horses to revitalize some of the teams, and a new mount for their scout.

A wagon train's expenses are paid by each individual member of that train. They've already spent a fortune putting their wagon and team—sometimes as many as six horses—together. Then there's food, clothes, other supplies. And when there's a problem, those people need to pay for their own repairs, or replacements. If they don't have the money, then they have to find it, or borrow it.

Some of the families on the train were together. When one wagon needed money, it got help from another wagon. In some cases, when a family could not afford its repairs, or replacements, its trip was over, and they had to settle right there.

This happened to five families, who had to be left behind. Clint wanted to pay their expenses, but on the days they broke down, they weren't near a town where he could get to a bank.

He didn't know why Major Tom Wallace had wanted to live with this responsibility. He didn't know how many families the Major had had to leave behind in all the time he was a Wagonmaster, but he knew he couldn't have done it. Just leaving those five behind weighed on his mind the rest of the trip.

***

They camped just outside of Salt Lake City, and some of the families began to discuss whether or not they wanted to settle right there. They brought their concerns to Clint that night, as a group.

"How much longer is this trip going to be?" one man asked.

"We have more than a month to go," Clint told him.

"I don't know if my family can put up with that," the man said.

"I have the same concern," another man agreed.

"You've come this far," Lyle Peters interjected. "Surely you want to see it through."

"We'll have to talk," they said, and went back to their wagons.

"They wouldn't have made it this far in the old days," Clint said, "when there were even more hardships."

"I believe it," Peters said.

"This is why there haven't been wagon trains west for years, now," Clint said. "And most people understood that the railroad took away these hardships. I'm still not fully understanding why these families chose to travel this way or why the Major would have taken it on."

"Wallace loved wagon trains," Peters said. "These last twenty years had been hard for him, since they faded out in the late sixties. When he heard that these people wanted to do this, he was on board immediately."

They were sitting around the fire, having finished their supper. Wilkie was off cleaning his cooking utensils.

"You know," Clint said, "I never asked you how you got involved?"

"I'm from Massachusetts," Peters said. "I've always wanted to come West. I was in my bank, making a withdrawal, when I heard the Stevens family discussing this wagon train. They and other families had planned this trip, but they needed a Captain, and a Wagonmaster. I'm an organizer, always have been. And I had met the Major years ago and knew what he used to do. It all just seemed to come together."

"Yes, but the trip from the East to Independence must've been hard for some families."

"People heard about this train being put together. They started calling it 'the last way west.' They wanted to be part of it, because members of their families had traveled this way years ago. And when a large contingent of Quakers got involved . . . some came from Massachusetts, some from Pennsylvania, some from Virginia . . . they all made their way to Independence and met the Major."

"And you?"

"I came with some of them," Peters said. "And the Major, he got Wilkie and Horton involved. Chuck and Dave, too. They had all worked with him before. Wilkie had driven chuckwagons on trail drives. Like I said . . . it all came together."

"The way I see it," Clint said, "this has to be the last one. Finally."

"These families," Peters said, "they were intrepid to have wanted to take this one, but they're not as intrepid as those families of the earlier trains."

"Well," Clint said, "we're lucky our final destination isn't California. I think they all would have quit well before then. Nevada, we'll probably make Reno with about half the wagons we left with."

"I need some sleep," Peters said. "I'll see you in the morning."

"Good-night."

***

Clint sat at the fire long after Peters had turned in, and after Wilkie had made him a pot of coffee and also called it a night.

He went over the conversation with Peters in his mind as to how the wagon train had come together. He still couldn't see why these families chose to travel this way. And he sure as hell didn't understand Peters' motivation.

Unless there were some other reasons the man wasn't talking about.

There seemed to be some connection between Peters and Stu Barnard. Barnard was the nervous type. It showed every time Clint came close to his wagon.

And somebody was following them. Of that he was certain.

But why?

Chapter Thirty-Six

The next morning, Clint and Wilkie went into Salt Lake City for supplies. Some of the families, who had decided to end their travels, went with them. When Wilkie and Clint returned from town, Clint figured they had about twenty wagons left. That was just half of what they'd left Independence with. These families certainly showed none of the fortitude that the travelers had shown twenty years ago.

That night both Liz Landers and Delilah Rogers approached their fire while Clint, Peters and Horton were being fed by Wilkie.

"Ladies," Clint said. "Would you join us for supper? Is there enough stew, Wilkie?"

"There's plenty," the cook said.

"Thank you," Delilah said. "We accept."

She and Liz sat at the fire, after the men moved to make room. Wilkie handed them both plates.

"You know," Delilah said, "we never tasted your stew until that night we had the communal meal. It was delicious."

Liz put some in her mouth. "And it still is."

"Thank you," Wilkie said.

"What brings you ladies to our fire this evening?" Peters asked.

Clint noticed that Horton couldn't take his eyes off Delilah.

"Well," Delilah said, "so many wagons have fallen by the wayside—"

"Many of them just decided to stop, and settle where they landed," Peters said. "Like here, in Salt Lake City."

"That concerns us!"

They all turned to the new voice, saw Abraham Stevens standing there with Ada and Ellie.

"In what way?" Clint asked.

"We're concerned with whether or not we'll make our destination," Abraham said. "Reno, Nevada."

"We'll make it," Clint said.

"With our wagons?" Liz asked.

"If you're all determined enough," Clint said, "yes."

"So, if all it takes is determination," Abraham asked, "why have so many fallen along the way like they have?"

"Because," Clint said, "they weren't determined enough."

"Or strong enough," Peters said.

"But you are," Clint said. "All of you. Aren't you?"

"Well, I am," Delilah said.

"Me, too."

"We are," Ada said.

Abraham looked at her.

"Yes, we are," Ellie said.

"Stay," Clint said, "and eat."

"We'll go back to our own fire," Abraham said. "We just wanted to . . . be sure."

"Consider yourself . . . assured," Clint said.

The Stevens family headed back to their own wagon. Ellie turned and looked at Clint over her shoulder.

"That girl likes you," Liz said to Clint.

"She's young," Clint said.

"I think the rest of the people we have on this train will make it," Peters said, "don't you?"

Clint decided to try something, to ease his curiosity.

"What about Stu Barnard?"

Peters stiffened just slightly, which was all Clint needed.

"What about Barnard?"

"Will he make it?"

"He will," Peters said.

"What's he got in his wagon?"

"The same thing everyone else has," Peters said. "His personal effects."

"Uh-huh." Clint finished the stew on his plate, passed the empty to Wilkie.

"Why ask about Barnard?" Peters asked.

Clint shrugged.

"Just curious," he said. "Wilkie, how about more coffee?"

Chapter Thirty-Seven

Clint walked Delilah and Liz back to their wagons.

"What was that about Barnard?" Delilah asked.

"Do you know him?"

"I know who he is," she said.

Clint looked at Liz.

"Same here."

"Something's going on between him and Peters," Clint said. "I'd like to know what it is."

"Well," Delilah said, "we could help."

"How?" he asked.

"Distract him, so you can get a look inside his wagon."

"You'd do that?"

"To help you?" Delilah said, taking his left arm, "of course we would."

"But," Liz said, touching his right arm, "first you have to do somethin' for us."

"Like what?"

They had reached Delilah's wagon by then, so they took his arms and led him to the back.

"Oh, now wait—" he said.

"We've waited long enough," Delilah said.

"Get inside," Liz ordered.

***

"What was that about Barnard?" Horton asked.

"I don't know," Peters said.

"Why would he ask that?"

"I don't know!" Peters said, again. "I'll go and talk to Stu."

"You do that," Horton said, standing up.

"What are you going to do?" Peters asked.

"I'm gonna ride out and have a look around," the scout said. "Make sure there's no danger out there."

"Okay," Peters said, also standing, "but then get back here."

"Right."

Horton went to saddle his horse.

Wilkie walked over to Peters.

"What do we do?" he asked.

"Nothing," Peters said. "I'm just going to check with Barnard. You stay here and wait for Adams to come back."

"Right."

Peters headed for Barnard's wagon.

***

Bob Horton rode out to where he figured Gentry and the other men would be watching the wagon train from.

"Gentry!" he called. Then he realized he was keeping his voice too low, which didn't matter. No one from the wagon train could hear him. "Gentry!"

He'd picked the wrong place.

He rode a little further, to the second place he thought they'd use.

"Gentry?"

"Here."

It was dark and moonless, but Gentry lit a match and Horton rode to it.

"What's going on?" Gentry asked.

"Can we build a fire?" Shelton asked. "I'm tired of cold camps."

"As long as it can't be seen from the wagon train," Horton said.

"How do we know that?"

"If you can see their fires, they can see yours," Horton said.

"Oh."

"But that doesn't matter," Horton said, and turned to Gentry. "I want you to come in tonight."

"Why tonight?" Gentry asked.

"Adams is suspicious," Horton said. "He's asking questions."

"So let him ask all the questions he wants," Gentry said. "Who's gonna answer him?"

"Well, nobody, but—"

"You're panicking'," Gentry said.

"What do you want to do?" Horton asked.

"The longest part of this trip is from here to Reno," Gentry said. "That's when we'll hit the train."

"And until then?" Horton asked.

"Business as usual," Gentry said. "Go back in and tell them nobody's out here."

"When you do ride in," Horton said, "I want Peters and Adams dead."

"What about the cook?" Gentry asked.

Horton shrugged.

"Hey," he said, "we're still gonna need a cook, aren't we?"

"Good point," Gentry said.

Horton turned his horse and headed back.

"Can we build that fire now?" Shelton asked.

Chapter Thirty-Eight

As Clint climbed into the back of the wagon with Delilah and Liz, the women began to undress him hastily. It had been some time since either had been with him. Delilah also pulled the cover over the entrance so nobody would be able to look in.

Clint had been determined not to be with either woman while on the actual wagon train, but their insistent hands and mouths had drained that determination out of him. As they peeled off his clothes, they began to kiss and touch him, and also divest themselves of their own clothes.

When all three were naked, any thoughts of resisting naturally disappeared.

They were on either side of him, and while Liz kissed his mouth and neck, Delilah kissed down his body, over his chest and belly, until she was nestled between his legs, nuzzling his hard penis.

As she licked his cock to wet it, Liz shimmied down and joined her, so now both mouths and tongues were on his groin.

He didn't know how long he was going to last, in the face of all this attention . . .

***

Lyle Peters found Stu Barnard sitting at his campfire, staring.

"What's your problem?" he asked.

"Nerves," Barnard said. "I told you my nerves was gettin' the better of me. I can't sleep. Plus, there's women on this train, and I ain't had a woman in months."

"Sorry I didn't think to bring any whores along," Peters said.

Barnard brightened at that thought.

"That woulda been good."

"No," Peters said, "it wouldn't have."

"Well, how about I ride into Salt Lake tomorrow, just for a poke? I'll come right back."

"Out of the question," Peters said, firmly. "We're leaving early in the morning."

"I'll catch up. I swear I will."

"Forget it, Stu. Look, we're on the last leg of the trip."

"Yeah," Barnard said, "the longest leg."

"You better relax."

"You got any whiskey?" Barnard asked.

"Jesus," Peters said, "I don't need you getting drunk! Get hold of yourself, man!"

"Yeah, yeah, okay," Barnard said. "Whatever you say."

Peters left Barnard to his staring, wishing he had been able to find a man with steadier nerves. At least Wilkie was keeping it together.

***

Delilah and Liz sensed that covering Clint's body with kisses—especially his penis—was bringing him close to the end, so instead they climbed up on him. Delilah took him into the steamy depths of her pussy, and Liz sat with her vagina on his face, and they did so while facing each other.

Clint had been in this position once or twice before, and as pleasant as it was, it was still a problem concentrating on all of the sensations at once. As he plumbed Liz's depths with his tongue, enjoying her sweetness and driving her to her climax, Delilah was bouncing up and down on his hard cock, driving him toward his own finale—which he didn't want to achieve too soon. Also, their energetic coupling had the wagon rocking back and forth, side-to-side, so that anyone passing would have to wonder what was going on inside.

Luckily, they were still the last wagon on the train, so the rocking went unnoticed.

***

Peters got back to Wilkie's fire, saw the little man seated there with his chin in his hands, elbows on his knees.

"Not you, too," he said.

Wilkie looked up at him.

"Whataya talkin' about?"

"Nerves?"

"Naw, I'm just tired. Stu suffering from nerves?"

"Yeah," Peters said, "a bad case."

"Shoulda hired somebody else."

"He was the last one we hired," Peters said. "If I'd known about his nerves, I would've kept looking, but we also had to get moving."

"I know it," Wilkie said. "If his nerves get too bad, we'll have to get rid of him."

"I know it."

"What about Horton?"

"What about him?" Peters asked.

"He's up to somethin'," Wilkie said.

"What makes you say that?"

"He ain't been complainin' lately," Wilkie said. "That makes me suspicious."

"Now that you mention it," Peters said.

"We better be real careful this last part of the trip," Wilkie said.

"I agree," Peters said. "Wholeheartedly."

Chapter Thirty-Nine

Delilah fought back a scream as Clint exploded inside of her. At the same time, Liz gushed all over Clint's face and chest and almost collapsed as her passion overtook her. The women came together in an embrace, then slid off of him. They turned and settled down on either side of him, and all three took the time to catch their breath.

"Oh my God," Delilah said.

"I know," Liz agreed.

"You ladies have to keep your promise, now," Clint reminded them.

"We will," Delilah said, "we just need to rest a bit."

"You want us to do it tonight?" Liz asked.

"Yes," Clint said. "I want to find out what's going on as soon as possible."

"What do you think's goin' on?" Delilah asked.

"I don't know," Clint said, "and I don't like not knowing."

"Who do you think is doin' somethin' wrong?" Liz asked.

"I don't know," Clint said. "Horton's been too quiet lately, and I know somebody's been following us. Only he doesn't seem to see them when he's out scouting."

"We're bein' followed?" Delilah sat up and grabbed a blanket to cover herself, as if someone was watching them, now. "Watchin' us?"

"From a distance," Clint said.

"But why?" Liz asked.

"Waiting for a chance to come in and take what they want," Clint said.

"To take what?" Delilah asked.

"Maybe I can find out," Clint said, "while you distract Barnard."

They all started to get dressed.

"How far do you want us to go with this . . . distraction?" Liz asked.

"As far as you want, I guess," Clint said. "He's not a bad looking man, right?"

"You want us to have sex with him?" Delilah asked.

"Hey," he said, "you offered to distract him. You must have had some idea how."

"Company," Liz said, "we were just thinkin' of keepin' him company."

"That's fine," Clint said. "Just get him away from his wagon."

"We can do that," Delilah said to Liz. "Right?"

Liz grinned.

"He's a man, isn't he?"

***

Clint, Delilah and Liz all left the wagon and walked back along the train. Most of the people had turned in for the night, one or two were still sitting at their fires, and waved.

When they were a couple of wagons away from Stu Barnard's, they stopped.

"I can see he's sitting at his fire," Clint said. "You two go ahead. I'll wait until you lure him away."

Liz giggled.

"What?" he asked.

"Lure him away," she said. "Makes us sound like hunters."

"Go!" he said.

Both women giggled and started walking.

***

Horton came walking back into camp while Peters and Wilkie were still sitting at the fire.

"I thought you fellas woulda turned in by now," he said.

"Just about to," Peters said. "Anything out there?"

"No, nothing. Where's Adams?"

"He went off with Rogers and Landers," Peters said.

"Yeah," Wilkie said, with a leer, "and he's been gone a while."

"He ain't so much," Horton said. "When do we get rid of him?"

"When we get where we're going," Peters said, "and not before."

"I can't wait," Horton said. "I'm gonna turn in."

"So are we," Peters said. "See you in the morning."

They all went their separate ways to bunk down in their bedrolls.

A few yards away, Mike Rowland crouched. When he saw the three men talking, he had decided to just wait and have a listen. Turned out to be a good idea. Apparently, those men had intentions of killing the Gunsmith when they all got to Reno. Rowland had to warn Clint Adams.

But then he thought, if Clint Adams died, what would happen to his horse? Somebody would have to take him.

He turned and went back to the horses. He needed to give this some more thought.

Chapter Forty

Barnard looked up from his fire as the two women approached. Staring into the fire had ruined his night vision for a few moments, but it didn't matter. He could see them very clearly, and he liked what he saw. One was dark and slender, while the other was full-bodied, and they were both smiling.

"Hello, ladies," he said. "What brings you here at this hour?"

"You do, handsome," Liz said.

"Yeah," Delilah said, "we wondered if you'd like to take a walk?"

He swallowed.

"With you?"

"Of course, with us," she said.

Neither woman had paid any attention to him this entire trip.

"Why me?" he asked.

"Well," Liz said, "to tell you the truth, you're the only man who's awake, right now."

Because his dick was getting hard just looking at them, this made sense to him.

"I'm game," he said, standing.

They approached him and each linked an arm.

"Then let's go," Delilah said.

***

It didn't take them very long at all to get Stu Barnard away from his wagon. Clint watched them walk off, then made his way over. Quickly, he climbed into the wagon, where there was already a lamp lit.

The inside was a mess, with dirty clothing every-where. The smell of rancid sweat was pervasive. At first glance, there was nothing there. He looked around, used the barrel of his gun to move some of the dirty clothing, open a trunk, but didn't find anything.

He holstered his gun and left the wagon, then walked around it on the outside. That was when he noticed the tracks the wheels left in the dirt seemed deeper than those left by other wagons.

He leaned over, looked under the wagon, then stepped to the back again. Now he saw it, and climbed back in. He knelt down, felt the boards that formed the floor of the wagon, and found a loose one. He looked around, found a knife, and pried the board up, then another. Sure enough, this was a false floor, and hidden beneath it was more than he expected. Actually, he didn't know what he expected to find, but he was surprised.

Guns.

***

The women couldn't find it in them to have sex with Stu Barnard. Neither could they force themselves to kiss him. But they did manage to back him up against Liz's wagon, and get his pants open. He actually didn't have a terrible penis. Not as pretty as Clint's, but big enough, and they took turns stroking it until he shot his seed into the dirt with a great groan.

"Jesus," he said.

Delilah and Liz looked at each other, wondering if they had distracted him long enough. Because they didn't know what they'd do after this.

***

Clint put the boards back in place, covered them, and got out of the wagon. He didn't know how long the women would be able to keep Barnard away.

He moved away from the wagon just in time, because at that moment Barnard came walking back, looking very satisfied with himself.

Clint worked his way back to Delilah's wagon, where the ladies were waiting.

"Was that long enough?" Delilah asked.

"Perfect," he said. "What'd you do with him?"

"You don't want to know," Liz said.

Since both women were drying their hands on a towel, he guessed. Why else would they have washed their hands?

"Well, I appreciate it," he said.

"What did you find?" Liz asked.

"Rifles," Clint said, "hidden in the floor of the wagon."

"Rifles?" Delilah asked. "But . . . why?"

"They're the new Springfields. They've got to be stolen, and obviously, he intends to sell them."

"To who?" Liz asked. "I thought the Indian wars were over a long time ago."

"They were," Clint said, "but they're not all happy with reservation life. But there are also plenty of white men who would buy those rifles."

"So Barnard stole them and is—what, smuggling them to Nevada?" Delilah asked.

"Barnard, and Peters," Clint said. "He's got to know about it."

"Anybody else?" Liz asked.

"I don't know," Clint said. "Horton may be in on it. Maybe Wilkie."

"And whoever you say is out there, following us?" Delilah asked. "Do you think that's what they want? Guns?"

"Could be."

"So what will you do now?" Liz asked.

"I'm not sure," he said. "We can just continue on tomorrow. Peters and Barnard and whoever else is involved, they're probably not going to do anything until we get where we're going."

"But . . ." Delilah asked.

"But I don't know about whoever's following us," Clint said. "They might make a move before then. I'll probably need help to fight them off."

"And you think Peters and Horton and others will help?" Liz asked.

"Oh yeah," Clint said, "because they could do it without revealing themselves and the guns."

"This sounds like you're playin' a dangerous game, Clint," Liz said. "You know, Delilah and I each have a rifle."

"I wouldn't want to put you ladies in danger," Clint said.

"If this wagon train gets attacked," Delilah said, "we're all in danger."

"Maybe," Liz said, "we should pass the word to some of the others."

"No, not yet," Clint said. "The less people who know what's going on, the more control I'll have. I don't want anyone acting before I'm ready."

"Okay, then," Liz said, "we'll wait until you give the word."

"But we're gonna be helpin'," Delilah said. "Count on that."

"I will," Clint said. "Believe me."

Chapter Forty-One

By morning Clint had decided what his next move should be.

Since he didn't know who he could trust on the wagon train—other than the women—he decided to keep his discovery to himself, for now. Even Chuck and Dave could have been working with Peters and Barnard to move those rifles to Nevada. He might have confided in Wilkie, since the little cook had worked with the Major for so long, but in the end, he decided not to.

The only other man he might have talked to was Mike Rowland. The fact that Eclipse got along with the man was almost enough of a reason.

But, as they pulled out the next morning, he did have Chuck and Dave continue to carry their rifles, and even suggested to Mike Rowland he keep his handy.

"This is the stretch of the trip I'd expect to find some trouble," he told them.

They all simply nodded and took up their rifles. He had the feeling he could trust them, but he still needed just a little more proof.

He watched Bob Horton closely, and noticed that the man was keeping to himself. Perhaps there had been a falling out between the scout and Peters. If there had, he might be able to use that to his advantage.

He continued to watch all the men closely.

***

A week out of Salt Lake, Clint realized there was something he missed. Wilkie's wagon was leaving deeper tracks than the others, just like Barnard's was. At first he thought it might have been because of all the chuck wagon supplies it carried, but then he decided there could have been more guns in that wagon. If there was, the little cook had to know about it. That meant he could forget about trusting him.

So he figured Peters was the mastermind, working with both Wilkie and Barnard. Horton could have also been involved, but it continued to look like the scout was distancing himself from the others.

He also noticed, when walking the train and coming to Liz and Delilah's wagons, that the two women had started carrying their rifles with them.

Clint decided to have a talk with Rowland. He didn't know the man well, so he could do it under the guise of wanting to get to know him better.

***

On that night, when they were a week out of Salt Lake, he was walking back to the front of the line when Abraham Stevens stopped him.

"What's going on with those women?" Abraham asked.

"What do you mean?"

"They've started carrying guns," Abraham said. "I noticed it a few nights ago."

"I think they're a little nervous, Mr. Stevens."

"About what?" he scoffed.

Clint thought a moment, then said, "Indians."

"What? There are no Indians out here."

"I explained that not all the Indians are happy with reservation life. So I guess they decided to arm themselves. It's actually not a bad idea."

"Do you think I should be carrying my rifle?" Abraham asked.

"Either that," Clint said, "or just keep it close." He patted the man on the arm. "Better to be safe, especially with your family to think of."

Chapter Forty-Two

On the eighth night outside of Salt Lake, Clint walked over to where Rowland was standing, rubbing down one of the team horses.

"You know," he said, "I never asked how you got involved in this crazy wagon train idea."

"I was the last one in, I think, just before you," Rowland said. "I came on board in Independence."

"So you're not old friends with any of these men?"

Rowland shook his head.

"I don't know them any better than you do."

"That's interesting," Clint said. "What do you think of them?"

"Who?"

"Peters. Horton. Wilkie, even Barnard."

"Hell, they're all right," Rowland said. "Well, except for one thing."

"What's that?"

Rowland stopped rubbing down the horse and turned to face Clint.

"They're plannin' to kill you."

"I figured that much."

Rowland looked surprised.

"You knew?"

"I suspected it."

"Do you know why?"

"I do."

"Why?"

Clint looked around.

"Can I trust you Mike?" Clint asked. "Because if I can, you're the only one."

"You can trust me," Rowland said. "Hell, Eclipse does."

"That's about the only reason I'm confiding in you."

"What's going on?"

Clint told him . . .

***

When he finished with his story and giving Rowland his own opinion about the men involved, he left the man standing near the horses, holding his rifle.

In camp he noticed, once again, that Horton was not there. Peters and Wilkie were sitting at the fire. They had all had their supper, already.

Clint sat and accepted a cup of coffee from Wilkie. He felt bad about the little man, because he had liked him. And now he might have to kill him.

"Where's Horton?" he asked.

"He rode out," Peters said, "Said he saw something."

"Tonight he saw something?" Clint said. "After so many nights of nothing?"

"That's what he said."

Clint dumped his coffee into the fire, causing it to flare, and stood up.

"What's wrong?" Peters asked.

"I think we're going to be hit."

"When?" Wilkie asked.

"Tonight."

Peters stood.

"By who?"

"Horton," Clint said, "and whoever he's been working with those who've been following us all this time."

"I knew he's been actin' strange!" Wilkie said.

"You sure about this?" Peters asked.

"No," Clint said, "but do you want to wait until I am?"

"No," Peters said. "What do we do?"

"Get your rifles," Clint said, "and find Chuck and Dave. Rowland, too. Meet me back here."

"Where are you going?' Peters asked.

"To warn everybody to stay in their wagons."

***

Most of the passengers wasted no time getting into their wagons, with their rifles, as Clint suggested.

"Pa, you should help Clint," Ellie told Abraham Stevens.

"But I—"

"No," Clint said to the man, "stay with your family."

Both Delilah and Liz wanted to help, too.

"You can help by watching this end of the train," he said. "And keep your rifles ready."

That seemed to mollify them, so they both got into Delilah's wagon together, since it was the last one in line.

***

When Clint got back to the front, everyone was there—Peters, Wilkie, Rowland, Chuck and Dave.

"What about Barnard?" he asked Peters.

"He wants to stay with his wagon."

Peters had probably *told* him to stay with his wagon.

"That's fine," Clint said. "We should have enough rifles."

"Shouldn't we spread out?" Chuck asked.

"They'll come here first, to get us under control," Clint said. "Then they'll go for the rest of the train."

"Are you sure?" Peters asked.

Clint stared at him.

"No," Peters said, "I don't want to wait 'til you are."

Chapter Forty-Three

Clint predicted Horton would come in first and try to get the drop on them. So he, Peters and Wilkie just sat at the fire, with Chuck, Dave and Mike Rowland behind Wilkie's wagon.

They were that way when Horton rode back in. He unsaddled his horse, left it at the picket line for Rowland to take care of.

"Where's Mike?" he asked.

"He's around," Peters said. "Did you find anything out there?"

"As a matter of fact," Horton said, drawing his gun and pointing it at the three of them, "I did."

Peters looked at Clint.

"You were right."

"What was he right about?" Horton asked. "Never mind, just drop your gun, Adams. And you two keep your hands away from your rifles."

"He was right that you were going to try something tonight," Peters said. "We all knew you were up to something, Horton."

"Yeah, well, looks like I got the drop on you, anyway."

"I don't think so," Clint said. "Take a look over there."

Horton looked around, saw Chuck, Dave and Mike Rowland step out, pointing their rifles at him.

"What's this?" he asked.

"Clint figured out your play, Bob," Peters said. "He was ready for you."

"Oh yeah?" Horton said. "Did he figure out your—"

"What's the signal?" Peters demanded, standing up. "To bring your friends in."

"What fr—"

"Come on, Horton," Clint said. "They've been following us for weeks, and you've been covering for them. Tonight's the night you were calling them in. How?"

"Guess," Horton said.

He was still holding his gun, so Clint walked to him and took it.

"There's only one way," Clint said. He walked to the campfire and picked up one piece of flaming wood. The look on Horton's face told him he was right.

"Tie him up," he said to Dave and Chuck, "then I'll wave this as a signal and they'll come in."

"And we'll be ready," Wilkie said.

"Right."

Chuck and Dave grabbed Horton, pulled him over to Wilkie's wagon and tied him to a rear wheel.

"Adams, you don't know—"

"And gag him!" Peters shouted. "So he can't warn them."

"You can't keep this—" Horton started, but Chuck stuck a bandana over his mouth.

Clint knew that Horton was trying to warn him about Peters, a warning he really didn't need. He would deal with Peters when they were finished with Horton's cronies.

"Okay," Clint said. "Here goes."

Clint stood next to the fire, which he assumed the force out in the darkness could see. He waved the piece of flaming wood he was holding over his head.

"Do you think they'll answer?" Peters asked.

"If they have a fire going—yeah, there it is."

Somebody out in the dark was waving a flame signal.

"Okay," Clint said, "get ready."

***

They heard the horses coming.

"If there's twenty men we're gonna be in trouble," Wilkie said.

"Six," Clint said.

"What?" Peters asked.

"Five or six."

"How can you tell?" Peters asked.

"Experience."

Peters looked around.

"Well, there are six of us. It should be even."

"It should be," Clint said, "but nobody fire until I do. Understood?"

They all nodded.

"All right, get into position. And tie Horton to a wheel on the other side, so they don't see him when they come in."

Chuck and Dave quickly moved him, and they got ready as the hoofbeats came closer.

***

Gentry led the men toward the wagon train, toward the first campfire.

"How do we know which fire?" Shelton asked.

"It's the first one," Gentry said. "Naturally. And that's where the signal came from."

"Yeah, okay."

"We just keep headin' for it," Gentry said. "When we ride in, don't fire until I do."

Chapter Forty-Four

Gentry and his men rode into the camp with their guns drawn. Clint was sitting at the fire alone, stood to greet them.

"Come on in," he said. "The coffee's ready. We've been expecting you."

"What?" Shelton said, looking at Gentry.

"Who told you to expect us?" Gentry asked, pointing his gun at Clint.

"Nobody had to tell me," Clint said. "You've been following us for weeks."

"How does he know that?" Shelton demanded.

"He's guessin'." Gentry said.

"No," Clint said, "your buddy Horton pretty much confirmed it. So if I was all of you, I'd put my guns down. Just drop them to the ground."

The six men looked around, saw only Clint, whose gun was still in his holster.

"He's bluffin'," Gentry said. "We kill him and the train is ours."

"And everythin' on it," Shelton added.

"There are rifles pointed at you right now," Clint said. "And not the rifles you were hoping to find."

"Jesus," Shelton said, "he knows about the—"

"Kill 'im!" Gentry said. His own gun had wavered a bit, so now he had to bring it to bear on Clint again, and that was his downfall.

Clint drew and put a bullet into Gentry first, knocking the man from his horse. At that point all hell broke loose, and the others started to fire. Peters and Wilkie fired from inside the wagon, while Chuck, Dave and Rowland stepped out from behind it and fired.

A hail of lead struck the remaining five men, who managed to get off a few wild shots before being knocked from their spooked horses. Several of the animals ran off, while the others simply moved away from the action, actually joining the picketed animals, where they felt safe.

Clint had fired several more times, so now he ejected his spent shells and quickly reloaded before checking the bodies.

"They're all dead!" he shouted.

Peters and Wilkie climbed down from the wagon. Chuck, Dave and Rowland lowered the barrels of their rifles, so that they were pointed at the ground.

"Anybody hurt?" Clint asked.

Peters looked around.

"No," he said, "that went perfectly."

"Okay then," Clint said, pointing his gun at Peters and Wilkie, who he had managed to keep together, by placing them in the wagon. "Drop your guns."

"What?"

"You heard me," Clint said. "I know about the rifles in Barnard's wagon, and there are probably more right there in Wilkie's. New Springfields."

"So what if we—"

"Drop your guns, and then we'll talk."

Peters and Wilkie looked at each other, then dropped their guns to the ground.

"What about us?" Rowland asked.

"If I'm right, none of the three of you are part of this."

Rowland looked at Chuck and Dave.

Chuck said, "Part of what?"

Dave just looked confused.

"Looks like you're right," Rowland said.

Clint spoke to the three innocent men.

"Peters, Wilkie and Barnard are transporting stolen rifles to Nevada, no doubt to sell."

"Wait," Peters said, "who says they're stolen?"

"Why are they hidden in false bottoms of two wagons?" Clint asked.

"To keep them safe," Peters said.

"You could've just loaded them into the back of a couple of wagons and told me about them. Instead, you chose to keep it a secret. They're stolen." He looked at Rowland. "Go and get Barnard, bring him here. Don't shoot him if you don't have to."

"Right."

To Chuck and Dave he said, "Untie Horton and bring him around. He was part of this, but he was double-crossing his partners."

They went to untie him, but came right back.

"He's dead," Chuck said.

"He's got a bullet in his back. It must have passed right through both back wheels."

"So," Clint said, "one casualty."

"And maybe two," another voice said, from behind him.

"Liz?"

"I'm here," she said, "and I'm pointin' a gun at your back."

"Delilah?"

"I'm here, too," she said. "She's pointing the gun at both of us, Clint."

"Drop your gun," she said to Clint, "or I'll shoot her first, and then you."

He hesitated, thought about turning and firing, but he didn't know exactly where she was, or exactly where Delilah was.

"You fellas drop your guns, too. Come on, don't take all day!"

Chuck and Dave looked at Clint for guidance.

"Drop them," Clint said, and tossed his gun to the ground.

Chapter Forty-Five

"Pick yours up," Liz said to Peters and Wilkie. They did so. "Where's Barnard?"

"Rowland went to get him."

"Well, be ready for him when they come back," she said. Then she spoke to Delilah, as Clint turned to face her. "Get over there," she said, with a push.

Delilah stumbled over and stood next to Clint.

"She pointed a gun at me as soon as the shootin' started," she said.

"So," Clint said, "you're the last member of this merry little band of gun runners?"

"I'm not a member," she said. "I'm the brains. This was all my idea."

"I'm impressed," Clint said. "A wagon train full of people trying to relive history. Meanwhile, you transport your guns in secrecy."

"And sell 'em to the highest bidder," she said, "Indians or whites."

"You still have to get them there," Clint said.

"Oh, you've brought us far enough that we can go the rest of the way."

"What about all of these people?"

"We don't need them anymore," she said. "We'll leave them behind, and they can go their own ways. We're not killers."

"So you're going to leave me behind, as well?"

"Oh no," she said, "we can't do that. You'll come after us. I know you well enough to be sure of that."

"What do we do with him?" Peters asked.

"Tie him up and put him in the wagon."

"And her?" Peters asked, indicating Delilah.

"We'll leave her behind with the others."

"And them?" Peters asked, indicating Chuck and Dave.

"Same thing. Leave 'em behind. But take their guns. In fact, take all the guns from the other wagons. But do it quickly, before they figure out what's going on. We don't want them banding together."

"Right."

"What's goin' on?"

They all turned and looked at Rowland, who had Barnard in front of him.

Liz turned quickly and fired her gun once. The bullet hit Rowland in the chest and knocked him onto his back.

"So much for not being killers," Clint said.

Peters, Wilkie and Barnard walked the wagon train and collected everyone's guns. Then they told each passenger, each family, to remain in their wagons or they would be shot. They succeeded in scaring most of them.

Ada and Ellie Stevens, on the other hand, got mad, while Abraham tried to control them.

"What did you do to Clint?" Ellie demanded.

"He's fine," Peters said.

"What are you going to do to him?" Ellie demanded.

"He's coming with us," Peters said.

"You better not hurt him!" Ellie said.

"Or kill him!" Ada snapped.

"Abraham," Peters said, "you better control your women."

"I will," Abraham said, "don't worry. They'll be quiet."

"Pa—"

"Quiet!" he yelled.

Both Ellie and Ada subsided.

Peters, Wilkie and Barnard carried all the guns forward to where Liz was still holding Clint and Delilah at gunpoint.

"Put those guns in Barnard's wagon," she told them. "We'll pick out the best ones and sell them, too."

"Right," Peters said.

"Then come and put Clint in this wagon and tie him up."

"What about me?" Delilah asked.

"If I put you in your wagon will you stay there?" she asked.

"No—"

"Yes, she will," Clint said. "Don't worry. She'll stay."

"Clint—"

"You're going to stay here with the other people," he said. "After we've gone, you'll all be able to move on."

"But what about you?"

"I'll be fine."

Delilah looked at the woman she thought was her friend.

"Liz, you better not kill him."

"Oh honey," she said, "I have other plans for him, don't worry."

Delilah looked at Clint.

"I want to go with you."

"Delilah—" Liz started.

"Let me talk to her," Clint said. "She'll go to her wagon."

"You better convince her."

"I will."

"You've got five minutes."

They put their heads together, and Clint told Delilah exactly what he wanted her to do.

"I'm ready," she said.

Liz told Barnard, "Take her to her wagon, and then get back here."

"Right."

She pointed at Clint and said to Peters and Wilkie, "Tie him up."

Chapter Forty-Six

They put Clint in Wilkie's wagon, and removed anything he could have used to cut his bonds. He had the rest of his night to try and get free and do something before they pulled out the next day. It was Liz's intention to leave with Wilkie and Barnard's wagons, with the rifles and Clint in them. No amount of argument—and he could hear them arguing—would convince Liz to either kill Clint or leave him behind.

"I want him," she told Peters. "That's it!"

Peters gave up.

It got quiet outside. Clint had to assume that they had turned in, but he also figured they'd leave someone awake to watch.

He just hoped they weren't watching too closely.

He remained awake, waiting.

***

He heard someone moving outside the wagon, along the side that couldn't be seen from the campfire. The canvas of the wagon moved, and he saw Delilah's face peering inside.

"Did you get it?" he whispered.

"Yes," she said, "right where you said it was."

She reached one arm under the canvas, and her hand was holding the Colt New Line he always kept in his saddlebags. Next came the knife that went along with it. She held onto it, and he scooted back so she could cut the bonds holding his hands behind his back.

"Okay," he said. "That's it. How many of them are outside?"

"Two," she said. "Peters and Wilkie are sitting at the fire."

"Do you know where Barnard is?"

"I think he's in his wagon."

"And Liz?"

"I'm not sure where she is."

"Okay. Back to your wagon. Quickly."

"Good luck," she whispered, and dropped the canvas down.

He hoped she made it to her wagon without being seen. He gave her enough time, and when he didn't hear anything, felt it was okay to move.

He left the knife behind, moved to the back of the wagon with the New Line in his hand. It held five shots. He was going to make them count.

First, he peered out, saw both Peters and Wilkie sitting at the fire. Wilkie's back was to him, but Peters was sitting on the other side of the fire. He wasn't going to be able to get the drop on them.

So he jumped out of the wagon, and as Peters saw him he grabbed for his rifle, yelling at Wilkie, Clint fired once. A well place small caliber bullet hit Peters right in the forehead, snapping his head back. He dropped as Wilkie turned with a panicked look on his face.

"Don't, Wilkie—" Clint started. Because he had liked the little man. But it was no use. As he started to bring his rifle up, Clint had no choice but to shoot him. One well-placed shot and he joined Peters on the ground.

"Now Clint had to move fast. He had to find Liz and Barnard before they could find him. Or worse, take hostages.

He ran to Barnard's wagon, got there as the man was climbing down.

"Stop there, Barnard!" he shouted.

"Jesus!" Barnard said, surprised. He had a pistol in his belt and went for it.

Clint shot him.

Three down, one to go.

He rushed to get to Delilah's wagon, passing all the others and shouting for people to stay inside, as they stuck their heads out.

But as he reached it, he saw he was too late.

Liz was standing there behind Delilah, with her gun pressed to the other woman's head.

"Why doesn't this surprise me?" she asked. "How did you get that gun? Did those idiots not search you well enough?"

"That doesn't matter," Clint said. "It's over, Liz. There's nowhere for you to go."

"Yes, there is," Liz said, "and Delilah will be coming with me."

"You can't take the two wagon loads of guns," Clint said. "All your men are dead."

"You'll drive one, while Delilah drives the other, with my gun to her head."

"The whole way?"

"If need be," Liz said. "I'm not letting this opportunity pass me by, Clint. Not after all these weeks."

"I tell you what," Clint said. "Take one wagon yourself and go. I won't stop you. I'll just take the rest of these people where they want to go."

"I could do that," Liz said, "but only after you load all the guns in that one wagon. And I'll take Delilah with me."

"Now that's not going to work for me," Clint said. "She stays here."

"And then you'll come after me. It may not be until you deliver all these people to Reno, but you will."

"Then we're at a stand-off."

"Or," she said, "you could come with me."

"That doesn't work for me," Delilah said.

"Shut up!" Liz said, digging her gun barrel into Delilah's temple.

"Shoot her, Clint," Delilah said, wincing. "Just shoot her."

"He won't take a chance of hitting you," Liz said.

"Liz," Clint said, "I can shoot you any time."

"Nice try," Liz said. "Tell me, after you shoot me, what would you do?"

"Bury you and your cohorts, take these people to Reno, deliver the stolen Springfields to the Army, and then be on my way."

"You've got it all planned."

"Yes," he said, "and it starts with shooting you. And I've killed enough people tonight that one more won't keep me awake."

"A woman?" she asked. "You'd shoot a woman, one you've been intimate with?"

"You're not just a woman while you're holding that gun on Delilah."

"What am I, then?"

"A target."

"A target you can hit?"

"Liz," he said, "I never miss."

"Well," she said, Delilah better hope you—"

Clint fired. The bullet went through Liz's forehead and into her brain, preventing her now lifeless hand and finger from pulling the trigger.

She dropped and Delilah ducked away.

"Jesus," she said, looking down. "You don't miss, do you?"

"Well, with this gun," he lied, "once in a while."

"Oh God," Delilah said, collapsing against him, when he came over to her. Into his chest she asked, "Can we still get to Reno?"

"Oh yes," he said. "We can and will. Let's go and talk to the others."

Coming October 27, 2019

THE GUNSMITH
452
Portrait of a Gunsmith

**For more information
click here:** www.SpeakingVolumes.us

On Sale Now!
THE GUNSMITH
449

For more information
visit: www.SpeakingVolumes.us

Coming October 15, 2019

Lady Gunsmith 7
Roxy Doyle and the James Boys

**For more information
click here:** www.SpeakingVolumes.us

On Sale Now!

TRACKER *series*
by Award-Winning Author
Robert J. Randisi (J.R. Roberts)

**For more information
visit:** www.SpeakingVolumes.us

On Sale Now!

MOUNTAIN JACK PIKE *series*
by Award-Winning Author
Robert J. Randisi (J.R. Roberts)

For more information
visit:

50% Off
Audiobooks

As Low As $5.00 Each
While Supplies Last!

Free Shipping
(to the 48 contiguous United States)

For more information
visit: www.HalfPriceAudiobooks.com

www.ingramcontent.com/pod-product-compliance
Lightning Source LLC
Chambersburg PA
CBHW030448250626
47154CB00003BA/1174